"Do you mind company?" Gabriel asked.

Leslie's eyes narrowed with suspicion.

He put both hands up. "I swear I just want to help."

"Fine. You can help," she said. "Just remember that there's a gymnasium full of students just steps away, so no funny business."

"I promise," he said, a wickedly seductive smile tipping up the corners of his lips. The moment they entered the school's storage room, Gabriel caught her wrist and spun her around, pinning her to the door.

"I didn't realize you were so gullible," he whispered against her lips.

Leslie returned his smile. "It looks as if it worked to my advantage."

Amusement glittered in his eyes as he brought his chest flush against her breasts. He lowered his head and took her lips in a kiss that had every fiber of her body humming with need.

If not for the door holding her up, Leslie would have melted into a puddle right on the floor. She pressed her body into his as he pushed his tongue into her mouth.

The moan that climbed from her throat was drenched with want.

"Gabriel, we need to stop," she murmured against his lips, but it was the exact opposite of what she wanted.

Dear Reader,

Have you ever visited a place and fallen instantly in love with it? So in love that you find yourself wanting to visit over and over again? And each time you visit you discover something new, exciting and unique that makes you want to keep coming back for more?

Well, that's exactly the way I feel about the fictional town of Gauthier, Louisiana. With every new book I write in my Bayou Dreams series, I find yet another thing to love about this charming town and its nosy, but well-meaning, residents.

Readers will recognize the heroine of *Forever with You*, Leslie Kirkland, from *Forever's Promise*. This widowed single mother definitely deserves her happily-ever-after, and I believe the young, handsome Gabriel Franklin is the perfect man to help her find it.

I hope you enjoy this latest glimpse into the lives of the people of Gauthier.

Happy reading,

Farrah Rochon

FOREVER WITH

You

Farrah Rochon

HARLEQUIN® KIMANI™ ROMANCE

Recycling programs
for this product may
not exist in your area.

ISBN-13: 978-0-373-86390-7

Forever with You

Copyright © 2015 by Farrah Roybiskie

For questions and comments about the quality of this book please contact us at CustomerService@Harlequin.com.

HARLEQUIN®
™ www.Harlequin.com

Printed in U.S.A.

Farrah Rochon had dreams of becoming a fashion designer as a teenager, until she discovered she would be expected to wear something other than jeans to work every day. Thankfully, the coffee shop where she writes does not have a dress code. When Farrah is not penning stories, the *USA TODAY* bestselling author and avid sports fan feeds her addiction to football by attending New Orleans Saints games.

Books by Farrah Rochon

Harlequin Kimani Romance

Huddle with Me Tonight
I'll Catch You
Field of Pleasure
Pleasure Rush
A Forever Kind of Love
Always and Forever
Delectable Desire
Runaway Attraction
Yours Forever
Forever's Promise
A Mistletoe Affair
Forever with You

Visit the Author Profile page
at Harlequin.com for more titles

For you, Mama.
Thank you for teaching me to trust and have faith.

Some trust in chariots and some in horses, but we trust
in the Lord our God.
—*Psalms* 20:7

Chapter 1

The frenetic whir of post-Sunday-service gossip floating through the Mop & Glo–scented air of the New Hope Baptist Church hall intensified the throbbing behind Leslie Kirkland's eyes. She slid into a cubby between the water cooler and a multitiered plant stand, her cheeks demanding a respite from the constant smiling at well-meaning church members determined to impart their gratitude for her singing at this morning's service.

Leslie took a sip of lukewarm fruit punch, the drink of choice during the church's fellowship hour, and glanced at her watch. She was counting down the seconds until she and her girls could leave without garnering judgmental stares from the deaconesses, who considered the fellowship hour sacred. She'd faced her share of raised penciled-in eyebrows when she walked into the sanctuary this morning after being absent the past two weekends. That was more than enough censure for one day, thank you very much.

"Leslie Kirkland, I swear you are an angel sent down from heaven."

Frustration at being discovered tightened the skin around her mouth, but her expression softened when she saw it was Nathan Robottom, owner of the hardware store in Gauthier, the tiny dot on the Louisiana map that Leslie had called home for more than a decade.

Nathan clasped her hands between his roughened palms and gave them a gentle squeeze. "That solo this morning was the loveliest thing I've heard since the last time you sang a solo in church."

"That's so nice of you to say, Mr. Nathan," Leslie said, her lips stretching into a genuine smile. It was impossible not to love this old man. "How is Ms. Penelope? I noticed she didn't join you this morning. I hope everything is okay."

"Aw, she's fine," he said, waving off Leslie's concern. "Her gout flared up and she didn't want to come limpin' in the church. She'll be sorry she missed your pretty singing." He gave her hands a good-natured pat before heading to the other side of the church hall where day-old doughnuts were doled out after Sunday service.

Leslie glanced at her watch again and decided that twenty minutes of fellowshipping should more than satisfy the deaconesses. She left her safe cubby in search of Kristi and Cassidy. Based on the trouble her daughters had given her when she'd woken them for church this morning, they should have been scratching at the doors to leave. As usual, they'd met up with friends and now she had to play Find the Kirkland Sisters.

As her eyes roamed the crowded hall, Leslie spotted Clementine Washington and Claudette Robinson sitting at the church ministries sign-up table. She averted her gaze, trying not to make eye contact, but she wasn't quick enough. The Two Cs rose from the table simultaneously and started straight for her.

What would happen if she made a run for it? Just dashed right through the doors?

"Leslie!" Claudette called, waving her arms to get her attention.

Too late.

"Ms. Clementine. Ms. Claudette," Leslie greeted with as much enthusiasm as she could muster. "How are you two doing this morning?" *Please don't ask me to join the Ladies' Auxiliary.* "I hope you're both doing well."

"Oh, yes. And especially after hearing you sing," Claudette said. "Girl, I know the spirit was moving in you."

"Amen," Clementine added.

"Thank you." She smiled. Leslie just knew her cheek muscles were on the verge of staging a revolt after the workout she'd put them through today. "Well," she said, clamping her hands in front of her, "I really need to find my girls. We have plans for this afternoon."

"Oh, I'm sure they're out there with the youth ministry," Claudette said. "Marsha and Lewis Marcel donated Popsicles for the little ones." She slid a step closer to Leslie and leaned toward her. "And speaking of people who live out on Willow Street…"

Confusion tugged at the corners of Leslie's mouth. *Huh?*

"Did you notice the way Sawyer Robertson was looking at you while you sang this morning?" Clementine asked.

Leslie couldn't prevent her eye roll even if the Eye

Roll Prevention Wizard had granted her special powers. And her eyes *were* rolling. Hard.

She should have known these two had something much more intrusive up their sleeves to ask her than joining the Ladies' Auxiliary. In the month since Sawyer Robertson had moved into the charming colonial on Willow Street—only a few streets from where she lived in the residential area of downtown Gauthier—Leslie had encountered no less than a dozen people who were all too eager to make introductions.

According to the gossip she'd overheard while browsing the produce section at the supermarket last week, the handsome divorcee, who had left Gauthier about three years ago, had just started a job with the state, though the gossipers had not been sure in what capacity. He hailed from one of Gauthier's more prominent families, and both of the ladies had agreed that he probably didn't have to work if he didn't want to.

Despite the town's small size, Leslie had never had much interaction with Sawyer in the years before he'd hightailed it out of Gauthier. She hadn't seen him much in the month since he'd returned, either, though she sure had heard his name enough.

"Sawyer comes from good people," Claudette said. "Rich as sin, but not uppity."

"Nope, never was uppity," Clementine agreed. "I went to high school with his mama, Cheryl Ann. Cancer took her a while back."

"Oh, I didn't know that," Leslie said. "Didn't his father die of cancer, too?"

She knew at least that much about him.

Clementine nodded. "Sawyer took care of Earl until he passed, then he sold the house, married that girl from New Orleans and moved somewhere up north." Clementine clucked her tongue. "Don't know what happened, but that marriage sure didn't last long."

"You know what I heard," Claudette started.

Leslie held up her hand. "This really isn't the place for that, is it? And I should really go—"

Claudette's face brightened. "Well, speak of the devil."

Leslie turned and just barely held in her groan at the sight of Eloise Dubois—another pillar of the church— and Sawyer Robertson walking toward them. Sawyer looked as though he'd been hit by a hurricane.

Or three very determined deaconesses.

"Look who I found in the parking lot," Eloise said.

"Why, Sawyer, you remember Leslie Kirkland, don't you?" Clementine asked in the most pathetic attempt at subtly known to mankind.

If only the floor could open up and swallow me...

Or, better yet, let it swallow up the deaconesses.

Leslie hid her frustration behind a smile as she stuck out her hand. "Nice to see you again, Sawyer."

The shimmer of understanding that flashed in his eyes put Leslie at ease. He sympathized. Of course he sympathized. They were in the same boat, being thrust together by a community of meddlesome, though well-meaning, people.

"It's nice to see you, as well," he said.

So, he had a really nice voice. And strong, yet soft hands. He wasn't bad on the eyes, either. His smooth dark skin was practically flawless, and those obsidian eyes practically dared you to look away from him.

But a pretty face had never been a selling point for her.

"I was sorry to hear about Braylon," he said. "All of

Gauthier was proud of him when he joined the military. He served our country well."

Leslie nodded and smiled. The old nod and smile had become her rote response whenever talk veered in the vicinity of her deceased husband.

"I really enjoyed your singing this morning," Sawyer added, his tone lighter. "It's been a long time since I stepped foot in a church. Your voice was a lovely homecoming."

He had that charm thing down pat. She was a sucker for a charmer, but still, no cigar.

"Thank you," Leslie said with another polite smile.

He shifted from one foot to the other. So did she. The awkwardness was so tangible that Reverend Allan would demand it add money to the collection plate if it hung around much longer.

Of course, it was hard not to notice the palpable awkwardness when the conversations around them had all but ceased, making it painfully obvious that she and Sawyer were the focus of every eye in the church hall.

Where in the heck were her daughters? She needed rescuing from this charming, handsome man before the dozens of people watching them—all of them failing miserably at being covert—got the wrong impression. Leslie knew that if even one person thought there was a spark between her and Sawyer, the sweet, well-intentioned matriarchs of Gauthier would wage an all-out campaign to get the two of them together.

Why couldn't the people in this town mind their own damn business?

It was as if a green light had been turned on the day after the first anniversary of Braylon's death. Once the acceptable grieving period had passed, all of Gauthier had been on a quest to find her a man, as if she was on the verge of collapsing from loneliness if she wasn't paired with someone soon.

Because, of course, she had all the time in the world to be lonely.

She was a single working mother with two daughters determined to take part in every extracurricular activity they could sign up for, and a full-time job that demanded more from her than she had to give. She barely had time to breathe.

But that didn't stop the fine people of Gauthier from foisting their single friends and relatives on her.

Sawyer Robertson was just one in a passel of men who had been paraded before her, all of them the *perfect* man to help her raise her poor little fatherless daughters. But Sawyer had proved to be more dangerous than any of the other men thus far. She had been introduced to her share of visiting nephews or friends of a friend of a friend, but the full-court press she'd faced since Sawyer's return was unprecedented.

And unlike the visiting nephews, Sawyer wasn't just passing through town. He was in Gauthier to stay. In a house just a few blocks from hers. All of Gauthier was determined to see this love connection happen.

This town! These nosy, prying people! She needed a break from it all.

"Mommy!" Kristi, her youngest, who had just turned five and was no longer her little baby, came running up to Leslie, the front of her white dress stained with purple Popsicle juice. "Mommy, are we still putting the swinging bed in the backyard after church?"

"Yes, we are!" And Kristi would get extra dessert for rescuing her from this painful situation. "Why don't you get your sister so we can leave?" Leslie turned to

Sawyer and explained, "It's a hammock. I promised the girls we would finally hang it today."

"Sounds like a lovely way to spend a lazy afternoon."

Yeah, that smile was *really* nice. There was no way to deny it.

"Do you need any help hanging the hammock?" he asked.

"Oh, no," Leslie said quickly. "The instructions are pretty straightforward. My girls and I can handle it."

A perfectly shaped brow arched before he asked, "Are you sure? I wouldn't mind coming over to help."

Leslie heard an excited gasp come from somewhere just over her shoulder. Lord, she needed to leave. Now.

"Yes, I'm sure," she said.

More silence. More awkwardness. More reasons to get the heck out of here.

She pointed to the double doors of the church hall. "I should probably go."

Sawyer nodded and stepped aside so she could pass. As she skirted around him, he called, "Uh, Leslie?"

Her eyes darted to him and she held her breath.

Please don't ask me out. Please don't ask me out.

Sawyer stuck both hands into his pockets and quickly glanced to the side where Eloise, Clementine and Claudette were staring openly. He lifted one shoulder in an indelicate shrug and said, "I was wondering if maybe you'd like to grab dinner sometime?"

Oh, good God. He asked me out.

The effort to keep the pained expression from taking over her face was a valiant one, but it was impossible to stop it. She mentally cursed every interfering busybody in this town. Sawyer was a perfectly nice man. He didn't deserve this.

"I'm sorry, but I can't," Leslie said. "I'm so busy

with work and my girls, and I'm also president of the PTO at the school this year. I just can't spare the time. Thank you for the invitation, though."

He did a fantastic job of hiding his disappointment, but Leslie still caught a glimpse of it in the way his mouth pinched at the corners.

She hated this. She hated being this perpetual stick-in-the-mud who constantly shot down advances from genuinely nice men. But finding a man was the very last thing on her agenda. She didn't care that the people in this town thought it was time for her to jump into the dating pool again. She was not putting herself out there until she was good and ready.

"Maybe some other time," Sawyer said.

Leslie didn't give him an answer, only another of those half smiles before she quickly made her way toward the door. She caught sight of Clementine, Claudette and Eloise standing off to the right. All three looked shocked and agitated, as if she'd messed up their well-laid plans.

That was too bad. She didn't need a matchmaker.

Unfortunately, she was living in a town that was chock-full of them.

Hammock hanging was not all it was cracked up to be.

What she'd anticipated to be a quick and easy project had turned into a quiz on deductive reasoning. Leslie lost track of how many times her eyes had darted between the creased instruction guide and the thick trunks of the two elms in her backyard. At one point she had seriously considered jogging over to that cute colonial on Willow Street and taking Sawyer up on his offer to help. But once she figured out the correct height—thus saving her butt from hitting the ground when she lay in it—it had been smooth sailing.

She'd spent the past half hour gently swaying in her newly hung hammock while Cassidy and Kristi attempted to play tennis in the backyard. It wasn't easy with Buster, the Yorkshire terrier Leslie had been bamboozled into adopting for the girls, stealing the tennis ball whenever she could get her little paws on it.

"You have to be quicker than that," Leslie called out to Kristi when the dog snagged the ball yet again. Her daughter plopped her hands on her bony hips and gave her a look that screamed *Duh, Mom*.

Chuckling at their plight, Leslie went back to the novel she'd been reading for the past month. She remembered a time when she could get through a book in a week. These days she was lucky to find twenty free minutes a day to indulge in her old pastime.

She'd become so engrossed in the book that it took her a while to realize that she had been steadily losing light. Leslie looked up through the branches overhead and noticed the ominous cloud directly above them.

"Girls," she called. "I think it's time to go inside."

There was a low rumble, then a loud crack of thunder. Just like that, the sky opened up and a deluge of hot rain poured down. Cassidy and Kristi both squealed as they raced to the back porch. Leslie swung the hammock to the right and tried to climb out, but it flipped over before she could steady herself, planting her right on the ground.

She groaned.

That was her, graceful as a swan.

By the time she made it to the back porch she was soaked. Kristi and Cassidy both pointed and laughed like a couple of hyenas.

"Well, thanks a lot," Leslie said. She wrung out her soaked shirt and flung the water at them. They both squealed again, jumping away from her. Buster scurried around the porch, trying to become a part of the game.

"Let's get in the house," Leslie said. "I'm starving."

Kristi pointed and giggled. "And wet."

"Oh, yeah?" Leslie wrapped her arms around her daughter, making sure to get her good and soaked with the dampness from her shirt.

After slipping the casserole she'd made before church into the oven, she, Cassidy and Kristi all took showers and changed into pajamas. It might not have been proper in some households to eat Sunday supper in pajamas, but it certainly was in this one.

As per their Sunday evening ritual, Leslie lifted the dry-erase calendar from the refrigerator and set it on the table. She wiped away the previous week's tasks and, handing the attached whiteboard marker to Cassidy, went through the schedule for the upcoming week.

"Don't forget Parent/Teacher Conference night," Cassidy said. "We get an extra star in English if our parents come."

The notion of bribing kids with stars in order to get parents involved in their children's school life was abhorrent, but Leslie knew it was also necessary. After all, just a year ago she had been one of those parents who routinely skipped school activities due to work obligations. Until she'd learned the price her absence had cost her daughters. These days she practically had her own designated parking spot at the school.

"I'll be there," Leslie assured Cassidy. She pointed at the whiteboard. "Make sure you have the correct times for softball practice. You don't want to be late again. And circle the Bayou Campers meeting so we don't forget."

Yeah, she had all the time in the world to be lonely.

Once dinner was done and the dishes loaded into the dishwasher, they settled in for their Sunday night movie. It was Kristi's turn to pick, which meant either *Casper the Friendly Ghost* or *The Lion King*. Leslie snuggled on the couch with her girls and watched *Casper* for the hundredth time. Once the movie was done, she declared bedtime, ushering the girls off the couch.

"It's Sunday night," Kristi reminded her. "We get a Daddy story."

Leslie ruffled Kristi's natural curls and smiled down at her, praying she was doing a good job of hiding her discomfort.

After going nearly a year hardly uttering her deceased husband's name, Leslie had slowly started reintroducing Braylon's memory into her family. It had been more difficult than she'd anticipated, but every Sunday night she shared with the girls a story about their father.

Seated on the edge of Cass's canopy bed, Leslie cradled Kristi on her lap, rubbing her hand up and down her baby's arms.

"Have I told you girls about the time your daddy tried to bake me a cake for my birthday?" Both girls shook their heads. "Well, your father was pretty good when it came to cooking hamburgers and hot dogs on the grill, but when it came to baking, he was horrible. He knew that I loved strawberry shortcake—"

"I love strawberry shortcake, too," Kristi interrupted.

"I know." Leslie tweaked her nose. "You get it from me. Your dad tried to make me a strawberry shortcake for my birthday once, but he couldn't find fresh strawberries so he used frozen ones. However, he didn't let them thaw out before serving me my piece of cake, so when I bit into the frozen strawberry, I hurt my tooth and had to go to the dentist to get it fixed."

Kristi plopped a hand to her forehead and moaned. "Oh, Daddy, Daddy, Daddy."

"Did the cake at least taste good?" Cassidy asked.

"I told him it did."

"Because you didn't want to hurt his feelings," Kristi guessed correctly.

"Yes," Leslie said. "But I made sure to order birthday cakes from the bakery every year after that. Aren't you girls happy I did?"

"Can I get a strawberry shortcake when I turn six?" Kristi asked.

"That's a year away," Cass pointed out.

"Wait. I meant tomorrow. Can I get a strawberry shortcake tomorrow?"

"Nice try." Leslie playfully tugged her curl.

She gave Cassidy a kiss and then carried Kristi to her bedroom. As Leslie tucked her in, Kristi put a hand on her cheek and said, "Thank you for tonight's story, Mommy. I like hearing stories about you and Daddy."

Emotion thickened in her throat. "I'm happy you're enjoying them," she said. "I know your daddy wishes he could be here to tell you stories, too."

She kissed Kristi's palm and then her forehead. Even though there was a night-light, Leslie left a crack in the door.

She made her way across the hall to her bedroom, tears on the brink of falling down her cheeks. But she sucked it up, straightened her spine and demanded they remain at bay.

It had taken a year before she'd stopped crying herself to sleep every night. Once she had, Leslie had made a vow to remain strong for her girls. She'd been on the verge of breaking down more times than she could count, but she was still standing.

And she would continue to do so.

Chapter 2

Gabriel Franklin stood before the science lab's Formica-topped table surrounded by nearly two-dozen wide-eyed fourth graders, who all stared intently at the stack of pennies, nickels and lemon-juice-soaked paper squares in the center.

"So, how many of you think we've made a battery here?" Gabe asked as he held a length of copper wire just above the stack of coins. Half the students raised their hands.

He eyed the doubters with an upturned brow. "That's all? The rest of you think I'm wrong?"

Anthony Radcliff's freckled forehead scrunched in skepticism. "It's just loose change and paper towels. How can that be a battery?"

Gabe tsked. "Oh, ye of little faith."

The crease in Anthony's forehead deepened. "Huh?"

"Never mind," Gabe said. "Gather around closer,

kids." He touched one edge of the wire to the penny on the bottom of the stack and the other to the nickel on top. "Now, check this out."

He connected the wire to an LED bulb and thanked the reliability of science when the bulb flickered and then shone with a soft glow.

The students erupted in cheers and excited howls.

"How'd you do that, Mr. Franklin?" Anika Reynolds asked in an awed whisper. "Is it magic?"

"It's science," Gabe answered. "It's exactly what we've been talking about for the past week, taking the negative charge of one metal and the positive charge of another, and connecting them with an acid. The penny is made of what?"

"Copper," the students replied in unison.

"And the nickel?"

"Silver!"

"And that lemon juice is filled with acid," Gabe said.

"So, can I make my iPod work with pennies, nickels and lemon juice?" Cassidy Kirkland asked.

"That would take a lot of pennies, nickels and lemon juice, but at least you get the idea." Gabe clapped his hands. "Okay, back to your seats. It's time to write up what we all just witnessed in proper scientific-method form."

He fully expected the grumbles and groans his statement elicited. He was only in his second semester of teaching at Gauthier Elementary and Middle School, but students were students no matter the school, and none of them enjoyed paperwork.

Using the electronic Smart Board that had replaced the green chalkboards he'd grown up with, Gabe went through the scientific method, going over the initial question he'd posed, the research the students had conducted, the hypothesis they all had agreed upon and the multitude of tests they'd run in order to investigate it.

He glanced over his shoulder and grinned at the sight of the twenty-two heads bowed over notebooks, their hands scribbling diligently. He required his students to take notes, even though the Smart Board allowed him to email whatever was written on it directly to their parents, which he also did at the end of every week.

The bell signaling the end of third period rang just as the students were finishing up.

"Remember your final topics for the science fair are due tomorrow," Gabe called above the bustle of zipping backpacks and desk chairs scraping against the tiled floor. "And if you're working with a partner, you *both* will need to turn in forms. It's not cool to have one person do all of the work, is it?"

That garnered mumbles and a few wisecracks. Also expected.

While the students filed into the hallway, Gabe returned to the rear of the classroom where the small but functional lab was located. He cleared the remnants of today's science experiment, washing the coins and leaving them to air-dry. Once the station was cleared, he packed up the battered leather messenger bag he'd been carrying around since his freshmen year of college, killed the lights and locked up behind him.

The teaching portion of his day was done. It was time to switch to his second role, interim assistant principal of Gauthier Elementary and Middle School—GEMS for short. The school officially had been renamed The Nicolette Fortier Gauthier Elementary and Middle School after the wife of the town's founder, but in the eight months that he'd lived here Gabe had yet to hear anyone call it by that name.

A month into his second semester as the fourth- and fifth-grade science teacher at GEMS, the school's assistant principal abruptly resigned. Gabe had earned his master's in education administration last summer, which put him in the perfect position to take over as interim assistant principal.

As much as he loved the classroom—seeing the kids' faces light up when he introduced them to yet another cool science construct was better than sinking a three-point winning shot at the buzzer—he loved this new role just as much. It wasn't as hands-on as teaching, but the opportunity it provided to affect the lives of an even greater number of students was worth the trade-off. He was in a position to change lives in the same way his own life had been change, but on an even *larger* scale.

The weight of all those tremendous possibilities being within his control was awe-inspiring. To anyone who had known him back in his early teen years, the idea of Gabriel Franklin even making it out of high school with a diploma would have been unfathomable.

But he *was* here. This was his life. He'd worked for it, reached for it, had done every single thing right for the past decade to make this happen.

The next step? Make that *interim* title a thing of the past.

Gabe had come up with a plan on how to do just that and in the past week had begun to put that plan in motion.

Just as he entered the suite of offices that housed the principal, assistant principal, school counselor and secretary, Ardina Scofield thrust a stack of folders into his chest. The secretary, whom Gabe had to admit kept this place running like a well-tuned engine, returned to her computer without a word of greeting. Gabe had learned the hard way that when you moseyed over to Ardina's bad side it was hell to get off of it. He'd found himself there after accepting an invitation from her to dinner and then backing out.

He should have known better than to encourage her advances, but she had approached him on the same day he'd struck out with the one woman—the *only* woman— who'd caught his eye since he'd moved to Gauthier.

Actually, to say he'd struck out wasn't entirely accurate. When it came to Leslie Kirkland, he hadn't managed to step up to the plate yet. Every time he even thought about broaching the subject of seeing his most dedicated parent volunteer outside of school, something told him to back off. It just never seemed like the right time to approach her.

He was tired of waiting for the right time.

And having dinner with Ardina in the meantime definitely would not have been the answer to his dating woes. Muddying the waters with a workplace affair was not on his agenda.

But Gabe knew he would have to figure out a way to get back into Ardina's good graces, because anyone who had worked in a school environment for any length of time knew that it was the school secretary who ultimately ran the show. They were the glue that held the multitude of parts together.

Gabe stared at her rigid back and considered clearing the air, but he'd tried that several times this past week and had only received the stink-eye in return. Until he came up with a better tactic, he'd steer clear of her.

Instead, he went the opposite way, backing into the

office that still had Assistant Principal James's name etched on the cheap plastic nameplate above the door.

Not for long, Gabe mouthed at the nameplate.

He deposited the stack of file folders on the desk and, after popping open one of the energy drinks he kept in his messenger bag, started on the mountain of paperwork that was an unfortunate part of his new job. Unfortunate but necessary. Every form he filled out was yet another opportunity to bring some much-needed changes to GEMS.

After a half hour of reading through proposals for new playground equipment, Gabe welcomed the knock on his door.

"Come in," he called.

Tristan Collins's face peeked through the narrow opening in the door. "You got a minute?"

"Sure. What's up?" Gabe asked his old college roommate, who was currently the band teacher at both GEMS and Gauthier High School. Tristan also had been the one to encourage Gabe to apply when the teaching position had opened up here just before the start of the current school year.

"I'm on my way to the high school, but I need to talk to you first," Tristan said. He looked over his shoulder before stepping into the office and closing the door behind him.

Gabe took note of the huge worry line creasing his friend's forehead. An uncomfortable feeling weaved its way through his gut.

"What's up?" Gabe asked again.

Tristan blew out an unsteady breath. "I overheard something in the teachers' lounge a few minutes ago. If it's true, you've got a problem on your hands. A big one."

* * *

"Something has got to be done about Gabriel Franklin."

Celeste Mitchell accentuated each word with a thump on the table, her balled fist rattling the collection of mismatched mugs of tea and coffee that had been consumed over the past hour. The treasurer of the GEMS Parent Teacher Organization, Celeste had called this emergency board meeting to discuss "alarming" news she'd just heard regarding the school's new interim assistant principal.

Simone Parker, the PTO secretary, hooked her thumb toward Celeste. "Look how this one's tune has changed. Just the other day she was talking about how cute Mr. Franklin's butt looked in his khaki pants, and now she's ready to run him out of town."

"He may be cute and all, but when he starts messing with my Lock-In, he's gone too far," Janice Taylor, the vice president, said.

"And there's nothing wrong with looking," Celeste argued. "I can be happily married and still look. Hell, sometimes Charles points them out to me."

"Can we get back to the discussion at hand?" Leslie asked.

She'd come straight from work to The Jazzy Bean, the coffee shop her sister-in-law, Shayla, had opened two years ago on Gauthier's Main Street. It quickly had become one of the most popular hangouts in town, and the normal meeting place when the PTO's board needed to discuss important topics outside the regular PTO meeting. Leslie wasn't sure when Gabriel Franklin's nice butt had made the important-topics list.

Not that she hadn't noticed the young teacher's nice butt. She had noticed it *way* more than she dared admit.

Leslie figured she was just one in a growing contingent of Gauthier females who had a crush on GEMS's newest teacher. As far as she was concerned, her little cougar crush was the safest crush in the history of all crushes. Not only was she too old for Gabriel Franklin, but there was also that other fact that could not be overstated. He was her daughter's teacher. Her. Daughter's. *Teacher.*

Safest crush ever.

"The Lock-In is our biggest fund-raiser of the year," Celeste said. "Do you know how tight our budget would be next year if Mr. Franklin canceled it?"

"And just what makes him think he has the *right* to cancel it?" Simone asked. "He got here all of two minutes ago and has the nerve to try to change the way we do things? I don't think so."

"I liked him better when he was just a teacher," Janice said. "It's when they put him in that assistant principal position that he lost his mind. Give a person a little bit of power and they think they run the place."

"You're right about that," Celeste said.

"I see it all the time," Simone added.

"Ladies, please." Leslie held up her hands and spoke as calmly as possible in an attempt to stave off the bevy of complaints being hurled at lightening speed. She waited until the other three ladies seated around the table quieted before continuing. "Everyone feels passionately about this subject, but if we all continue to talk over each other, we'll never get this figured out."

"What's there to figure out?" This from Celeste. "We all can see what's going on here. Mr. Franklin has decided that *he* knows what's best for *our* children. Barely a child himself," she finished with an aggravated huff.

"That's what I'm talking about." Simone pointed her

mug at Celeste. "He can't be more than twenty-five. What makes him think he knows better than the rest of us?"

"I heard that he taught for a few years in New Orleans before coming to Gauthier," Leslie said. "He has to be older than twenty-five."

"Fine, twenty-six, then," Simone retorted after taking a sip of tea.

"I don't care how old he is or how cute he is," Janice said. "What I care about is the Lock-In. I've personally worked my butt off to make it a success, and I don't appreciate someone who just moved here thinking he can come in and change the way we've been doing things for years. We need to figure out how to handle this problem."

"First, we need to make sure there actually *is* a problem," Leslie reminded them. "It's all hearsay at this point."

Although, if the news Celeste had shared turned out to be true, they definitely had a problem on their hands. Actually, GEMS's interim assistant principal was the one with the problem. Threatening the PTO's major fund-raiser was the equivalent of swinging a bat at a nest of angry hornets.

"Well, someone needs to approach Mr. Franklin so that we can get to the bottom of this." Janice pointed to Leslie. "I think you should do it."

"Me?" Leslie yelped. "Why me?"

"Because you're the PTO president. It's your job."

Great.

Leslie wouldn't say she'd been railroaded into the PTO president position, but she had not been the most willing candidate. She'd caved under the mountain of guilt at having <u>missed</u> so many volunteer days last year.

She'd accepted the position because, for the most part, being the PTO president at Gauthier Elementary and Middle School was an easy job.

Until Gabriel Franklin had decided to rile up every parent in the entire school.

Leslie splayed her fingers over her forehead and massaged her temples.

"So, when are you going to meet with him?" Simone asked.

"Yeah, Leslie, when?" Janice piped in. "It needs to be soon, before he decides to change something else."

"Exactly!" Celeste pounded on the table for emphasis. "You need to tell Mr. Franklin how we do things around here."

There was a light rapping on the wall before Leslie's sister-in-law, Shayla, peeked around the divider that had been added to the rear section of The Jazzy Bean to create the illusion of a separate meeting room.

"Excuse me, ladies," Shayla said softly. "I hate to intrude, but do you mind keeping it down? A few of the college kids are studying. It's midterms."

"We're sorry," Leslie said. "Please apologize to them. We promise not to get too loud again."

Shayla sent her an understanding smile before going back into the main part of the coffee shop.

"Look," Leslie said. "Before I approach Mr. Franklin I will need all the facts surrounding the supposed cancellation of the Lock-In. Nothing official has been sent home with the students."

"But Ardina said she heard Mr. Franklin and Mr. Williams talking about it in his office."

"We can't rely on Ardina's word alone," Leslie said.

"Why not?" Celeste asked. "Ardina knows everything that goes on at that school. Nothing gets past her."

"I think Leslie is right," Janice said. "The PTO shouldn't approach Mr. Franklin with this until there's some type of official announcement."

Finally, someone talking some sense!

Janice turned to her. "But you can still approach him *off* the record. Tomorrow night is Parent/Teacher Conference night. You need to take Mr. Franklin aside and find out exactly what he's up to."

"That's a good idea," Simone said.

"Yes, do it," Celeste added.

"Wait, wait, wait." Leslie's hands went up again. "Didn't we just agree that we shouldn't do anything until we're sure he's made an attempt to cancel the Lock-In?"

"You know how these people operate," Janice said. "He and Mr. Williams are probably scheming behind the scenes this very second, coming up with a bunch of reasons to cancel it. They're going to just throw it on us at the last minute without giving us a chance to make our case."

"I can't believe Mr. Williams would go along with this," Celeste said. "He knows how much the money we make from the Lock-In helps with the activities the PTO puts on throughout the year."

"I don't want to sound disrespectful or anything," Simone said. "But Mr. Williams is getting up there in age. Who knows what kind of fast talk Gabriel Franklin is using on him?" She turned to Leslie. "You need to take care of this."

"Why do *I* have to be the one who approaches Mr. Franklin if it isn't in an official PTO capacity?" Leslie asked. "Any one of you can do it."

"Because you're better at this than we are," Simone said.

If that isn't the biggest load of bull.

"And you have to meet with him anyway since Cassidy is in his class," Janice said.

"So is Willow," Leslie pointed out, speaking of Janice's daughter, who was also one of Cassidy's best friends.

"Yeah, but she's struggling in science. Our conversation will be uncomfortable enough as it is."

"Come on. You can do this, Leslie," Celeste encouraged. "We need the lowdown on his motives."

"Yeah, who knows what he's trying to do. He may be—"

Leslie put up a hand, cutting off Simone before she could voice whatever nefarious plot had popped into her head. "I think we've had enough speculation for one night," she said. If they weren't careful, by tomorrow there would be a rumor that Gabriel Franklin was trying to dismantle the entire PTO.

"I'll talk to him." Leslie finally capitulated.

"While you're at it, ask him about these drills he's set up for the fourth-grade class, too," Janice said. "The kids have enough homework."

"That's to help them prepare for the state test," Leslie said. "You can't fault him for wanting the kids to be extra prepared."

Shayla peered around the dividing wall again.

"We were just wrapping up," Leslie told her before she had the chance to speak. "No need to throw us out."

"I wasn't going to throw you all out," Shayla said with a laugh.

"You have Zumba tonight, don't you?"

The Zumba lessons Shayla began teaching at The Jazzy Bean last year had become so popular that a third night had to be added to meet the huge demand.

"So maybe I *was* coming to throw you all out," her sister-in-law said. "But I also wanted to make sure no one needed anything from the kitchen. Lucinda is shutting down in just a few minutes, so if you have any requests this is your last chance to get them in."

"I need to get home and do some cooking of my own," Simone said. "My boys will be getting in from baseball practice soon, and if the steaks I left defrosting aren't cooked, they'll eat 'em raw."

"Teenage boys are ridiculous, aren't they?" Celeste said. "Our monthly grocery bill is almost as much as the mortgage. Be grateful you have girls, Leslie."

"My problem is getting my five-year-old to eat anything, but I don't want your problems, either."

Leslie remained seated at the table they'd occupied for the past hour while the other three ladies packed up their things. Once they were gone, she dropped her head on the lightly distressed wood and thumped it several times.

"Why? Why? Why?" she said over and over again.

"Aw, you poor thing." Shayla said. "If the volume of their voices was any indication, it sounds as if things got a bit heated. What's going on?"

"GEMS's new assistant principal is making a nuisance of himself."

"I didn't even know there was a new assistant principal. What happened to Mr. James?"

"He's off to Australia. You didn't hear about that?"

"No," Shayla said, taking the seat Celeste had occupied. "When did this happen?"

"About a month ago. Where have you been?"

A lazy smile stretched across Shayla's lips.

"Never mind." Leslie laughed. "I know where you've been. The honeymoon phase is nice, isn't it?"

"Heavenly," Shalya said. "If I had known married life was so nice I would have tried it years ago. But back to Mr. James. What's he doing in Australia?"

"His wife got a huge job promotion but it required her to transfer to Melbourne. Mr. James put in his resignation and they were gone within days. They've moved the new science teacher into the assistant principal position for now. He's doing double duty, because he's still teaching."

And making her life more complicated than necessary.

"That's Mr. Franklin, right? Cassidy loves him. She was just telling me about some experiment they did using balloons and empty water bottles."

"He's a great teacher, but he's not making many friends as an assistant principal. There are rumors that he wants to cancel the school Lock-In," Leslie explained. "It's the PTO's biggest fund-raising event and, needless to say, some parents are not happy about this."

"Back up a sec. What's a lock-in?"

"You really are out of touch, aren't you?"

"I've been in the coffee business for the last twenty years. I am completely clueless when it comes to this stuff. Now, what's this lock-in thing?"

"It's an event at the school where students are locked in the gymnasium overnight. There's food, movies and games. Many of the kids stay up the entire night."

Shayla grimaced and scrunched her shoulders in an exaggerated shudder. "Sounds noisy."

"It is." Leslie laughed. "But the kids love it. And they spend lots of money in that twelve-hour period. The money raised from last year's Lock-In accounted for over half of the PTO's funds last year."

"So why does Mr. Franklin want to cancel it?"

"I don't know if he wants to cancel it or not. Until I hear it directly from him it's still just a rumor. But I need to find out if there is any truth to it." Leslie sighed and took a sip of her caramel latte. "As president of the PTO, the other members of the board expect me to approach Mr. Franklin."

"Ah." Shalya nodded, then frowned. "How did you become PTO president again?"

"Don't ask."

Shayla barked out a laugh. "You poor thing. Why don't you let me treat you to an early dinner? It sounds as if you've earned it."

"Thanks, but I can't. The girls' babysitter asked me to be home by seven."

"Oh, how is she working out?"

"She's only watched them a couple of times, but Kristi is already in love with her. Cass, on the other hand, misses coming over to her auntie Shayla's after school."

Shayla slapped a hand to her chest. "Don't. I feel guilty enough as it is that I can no longer watch them after school."

"Oh, stop it," Leslie said. "You know I'm just teasing. You'll be able to watch them for me tomorrow, though, right? It's Parent/Teacher Conference night at the school."

"Of course," Shayla said. "Xavier is more excited than I am. He just bought a bunch of board games. He's going to be so disappointed when all Kristi and Cass want to do is watch YouTube videos of cats doing tricks."

Shayla had married Dr. Xavier Wright a few months ago. A transplant from Atlanta, Xavier had settled into life in Gauthier much easier than Leslie had when she'd first moved here. He'd charmed the pants off everyone in town, including her sister-in-law.

Shayla plopped an elbow on the table and rested her chin in her upturned palm. "Sooooo," she said, stretching the word out in a singsongy voice. "What's this I hear about you and Sawyer Robertson chatting after church?"

"Oh, please don't start," Leslie said. She pushed up from the table.

"I just want to know what was said." Shayla whined. "Come on, Leslie. This is huge."

"No, it's not. And I hope the nosy, meddling people in this town will just let it go."

Shayla caught her wrist, halting her exit. She waited until Leslie turned to face her before she asked, "Is it that you're just not ready to date yet?"

Leslie's eyes fell shut. "I just…" But she didn't know how to put what she was feeling into words. So she went with the easiest cop-out. "Yes. I want to take my time," she said. "And I don't need the pressure of knowing that everyone around here is looking at my every move."

"Okay, okay," Shayla said. "I will put the word out that everyone needs to back off."

"Including my well-meaning sister-in-law?"

"Do I have to?" Shayla pouted. Leslie just stared at her. "Oh, okay," Shayla grumbled. "No more talk about Sawyer, even though he was at one time considered the biggest catch in Gauthier. Used to drive us girls crazy back in high school. He's also—"

"Shayla!"

"Sorry," she said. "Anyway, since you won't allow me to take you out to dinner, at least let me order a pizza so you don't have to cook tonight."

"I can order a pizza."

"Can I at least pay for it?"

Even though their once-stony relationship had vastly improved over the past year, there was one area where she and Shayla still butted heads. Leslie had lost count of the number of times she had to remind her sister-in-law that she and the girls were not her financial responsibility. They both knew that her late husband's pension from the Army didn't cover much. And, even though she made decent money as a financial analyst, raising two daughters on her own was an expensive undertaking.

But they were not in dire straits. Not even close. She'd saved well over the years, and because they lived in Braylon and Shayla's childhood home, she didn't have a mortgage. She could pay for a pizza.

But she didn't want to argue with Shayla, and Leslie knew if she turned down her sister-in-law's offer it would turn into a skirmish.

"Make sure you order one half with just cheese," she told her. "Kristi has decided she no longer eats meat."

"I love that kid," Shayla said.

"And thanks again for putting up with our little impromptu meeting."

"You know you all are welcome anytime. Just tell Celeste to use her inside voice next time."

Laughing, Leslie hugged her good-night before Shayla retreated behind the counter. Leslie picked up a couple of oatmeal-and-cranberry cookies from The Jazzy Bean's healthier sampling of baked goods. If they were having pizza tonight she might as well go all out and let the girls have dessert, too.

Even though she lived within walking distance of Shayla's coffee shop, she had driven here straight from the office. She backed out of the slanted parking spot and in less than five minutes pulled into the driveway of the house she'd lived in since marrying Braylon eleven years ago. A part of her was happy to have her daughters growing up in their father's childhood home, but there was another part of her that dreaded walking through the door.

It had been an ongoing struggle for nearly two years. Being in that house surrounded by memories of a husband who was no longer here, a life that no longer existed, was nothing short of torture. Some nights it took every ounce of strength she possessed just to find the courage to fall asleep in her own bed.

Which was why Leslie had finally decided to put action to the thoughts that had been swirling in her brain for the past couple of months. She had requested a meeting with her boss and was going to ask for a transfer to the company's Houston office.

Leslie closed her eyes and sucked in a deep breath. "The girls will like Houston," she said to the empty car.

It would be nice if she really believed that.

She had grown up in Houston, and even though it was only six hours away by car, she only went home about once a year. It hadn't always been easy growing up in those rough inner-city streets. But at least Houston wasn't filled with so many heartbreaking memories. Braylon's death had created a pall over just about everything that she had grown to love about Gauthier over the years. She needed to break free from it all.

Leslie grabbed her laptop bag from the trunk and entered the house through the side door that led to the kitchen. The moment she walked in, her legs were surrounded by bony five-year-old arms.

"Mommy!" Kristi exclaimed. She pulled away and looked up at Leslie with those deep brown eyes that looked so much like Braylon's. "Why are you just getting home? It's already dark."

"I'm sorry, sweetie." Leslie pulled at one of her bouncy curls. "Mommy had a late meeting at work, and then I had to meet with a couple of other mommies at Auntie Shayla's restaurant."

"Cassidy said it's a coffee house and café, not a restaurant."

"Well, excuse me," Leslie said. "I had a meeting at Auntie Shayla's coffeehouse and café. Where's Cass?"

"In the living room. She's teaching Brittany how to twerk."

"What?"

Leslie tossed her bag on the kitchen table and rushed to the living room. She found Cassidy and Brittany Meyer, the sixteen-year-old babysitter she'd hired a few weeks ago, in the middle of the living room with their hands on their thighs and their rear ends in the air, gyrating like a couple of washing machines. Buster made figure eights between their legs.

"Excuse me, but what is going on here?" Leslie called over the music.

"Hey, Mom," Cassidy said.

"Hi, Mrs. Kirkland," Brittany said with a wave.

"What's going on here?" Leslie asked again, pointing to the television that had a YouTube video of someone giving instructions on how to do the dance move that Leslie had expressly forbidden either of her girls from doing.

She turned to face the girls and folded her arms over her chest. "You know the rules, Cassidy. This is a no-twerking household."

"But Brittany said that white girls can't twerk, so I

wanted to show her that she could learn to twerk if she really wanted to."

Lord, help her.

"Sorry, Mrs. Kirkland," Brittany said. She pointed the remote at the TV and the screen went black. "I didn't know about the no-twerking rule."

"No twerking and no playing with the stove," Kristi said, eating the oatmeal cookie that was supposed to be dessert.

"It's okay," Leslie said, waving off Brittany's concern. "I didn't think I needed to say anything, since these two already knew about the rule." She gave Cassidy and Kristi another stern look as she handed Brittany a twenty-dollar bill. "Thanks for staying a little later today."

"No problem. I'm sorry I can't watch them for you tomorrow."

"Don't worry about it. The girls will be going to their aunt's."

"We're going to Aunt Shayla's tomorrow?" Kristi asked, jumping up and down in excitement.

Leslie walked Brittany to the front door just as the pizza deliveryman was pulling up. There were more excited screams at having pizza for dinner.

Other than the dozen times Leslie had to reprimand Kristi for trying to feed Buster pepperoni—she'd apparently turned back to a carnivore overnight—dinner went off without incident. By the time they were all fed and showered, Leslie was dead on her feet, but it still would be a few hours before she could crawl into bed. She had a ton of work she'd been forced to bring in from the office.

She was so determined to do it all, but Leslie knew

this superwoman thing was nothing but a facade. She couldn't do it all. And if she didn't slow down, sooner or later, she was going to pay for it.

Chapter 3

Her arms crossed over her chest, Leslie meandered around the science lab as she waited her turn with Cassidy's science teacher at GEMS's Biannual Parent/ Teacher Conference night. The first conference of the year, which had been scheduled in the fall, had been preempted by a tropical storm that veered toward the Mississippi coastline just before making landfall, but still caused heavy flooding in Gauthier and surrounding towns. For some parents tonight would be the first time they got the chance to meet with teachers this school year.

An official event wasn't necessary for parents and teachers to meet and discuss school happenings. Leslie would guess that most parent/teacher conferences took place in the grocery store or the bank or the pharmacy. The majority of the teachers at GEMS had lived in Gauthier their entire lives. They'd gone to high school with Braylon, or they attended the same church, or they were regulars at Shayla's coffeehouse. It was the nature of living in a small town.

And then there was Gabriel Franklin. The outsider.

He wasn't the first nonlocal to teach at GEMS, but the handful of teachers who had come to Gauthier from other cities had blended in rather easily and didn't make many waves.

Mr. Franklin had begun procuring his reputation as a skilled but demanding teacher just a few days into his first week at GEMS. He had challenged the students—and thus the parents—by requiring more time at the dinner table doing homework. It had been a shock to everyone's system.

Some parents had complained, but others had agreed that Mr. Franklin's way of teaching would help the children in the long run. The fact that he was a bit of a charmer hadn't hurt, either. He'd won over half the hearts in Gauthier during the first PTO meeting of the year, when he'd given an impassioned plea to the parents, daring them to push their children so they could meet their fullest potential.

That was probably the same time Leslie's little harmless infatuation with him had begun. She figured it had started because he'd come along around the same time she had made the decision to become more active at the school. His enthusiastic teaching style and the devotion he showed to each student were inspiring. This was not just a job to him. Gabriel Franklin cared about the work he did. He was everything Leslie wanted her daughter's teacher to be.

He was also smart and cute and young and off-limits.

She had never been bold enough to ask, but Leslie figured he had to be in his late twenties. A smart, cute twentysomething-year-old teacher who probably spent his weekends partying in New Orleans didn't go for a midthirtysomething-year-old widow with two children and a dog.

So, yes, her silly little crush on the cute Mr. Franklin was also a very safe crush, because Leslie knew she could never date her daughter's teacher.

She glanced toward the front of the classroom where he was currently speaking with Sadie and Michael Crumb, parents of Gauthier's infamous set of triplets, Micah, Michelle and Michael Crumb Jr. From what Leslie had heard, the triplets were a handful. According to Cassidy, the Crumb children thought they were hot stuff because they had made it into the local paper. Her daughter was now determined to do something even grander than being born on the same day as her siblings so that she could have her picture in the paper, as well.

If the intense body language was any indication, Mr. Franklin and the Crumbs would not be done anytime soon, so Leslie continued her tour of the classroom. It looked as if there had been a lot more activity since she last visited a couple of weeks ago.

Her eyes wandered over the collection of petri dishes, each with various amounts of bacteria growing inside of it. She suspected that this project was the reason behind Cass's sudden insistence that everything in the bathroom and kitchen be wiped down completely before they went to bed at night. Mr. Franklin had put the fear of mold spores into her daughter's heart, and everyone in the house had to suffer the consequences.

Leslie ambled over to the rear of the classroom where glossy posters of the steps of the scientific method, the effects of erosion and diagrams of the food chain hung on the wall next to several snapshots of the students exploring the boggy edges of the Bogue Falaya River during last month's field trip. She had joined them as a chaperone for that adventure. She was still finding mud in places where mud shouldn't be.

She peered inside the huge terrarium on the counter that spanned the back wall and jumped back when a praying mantis poked his head out from behind a rock.

"Mrs. Kirkland?"

Leslie jumped again. She pivoted and found Gabriel Franklin right behind her. She took a startled step back and nearly lost her footing.

"I'm sorry." He reached out and grabbed hold of her arm. "I didn't mean to frighten you."

"That's okay." Leslie flattened her palm against her chest and sucked in a deep breath. "Just give me a minute." Straightening, she expelled a shaky laugh. "I was so engrossed in looking around the classroom. A lot has changed since my last visit."

"That's right. You haven't been here in a few weeks. Remind me to show you the new microscope once we're done. By the way, I'm sorry about that last meeting running a little long," he said over his shoulder as they walked back to the front of the classroom.

"There's no need to apologize. I can understand why the Crumbs need a little extra face time."

"Yes, the Crumb children." He shook his head and let out a deep chuckle. "They are a rather, uh, unique bunch." Perching a hip on the edge of his desk, he motioned for her to take a seat in one of the plastic blue desk chairs.

As she slid onto her seat, Leslie reminded herself that this very nice man with this very nice smile was her daughter's very young teacher. *Her daughter's teacher.*

But he did have a *very* nice smile. He had a slightly

crooked front tooth that gave his face just the right touch of personality. His gold-toned skin stretched over enviably high cheekbones and a strong, square chin. And that wavy jet-black hair looked so soft that her fingers itched with the need to run through it. Between Sawyer Robertson and Gabriel Franklin she was racking up the encounters with pretty men this week, wasn't she?

He cleared his throat and said, "Uh, Mrs. Kirkland?"

Leslie's neck stiffened in shock as she tore her attention away from his full lips—lips that were now curved in a slight grin.

Had he caught her staring?

His dark brown eyes sparkled with amusement as he cleared his throat again. Yes, he had. The faint blush that stole over his fair skin erased all hope that she had not embarrassed the both of them by ogling his lips as if they were a dessert buffet.

No words could describe this level of mortification. She would trade her entire James Lee Burke hardback collection in exchanged for a chilled towel to cool her heated cheeks.

Leslie curled her fingers around the edge of the desk and forced herself not to find something else in the room to stare at. If she didn't maintain eye contact she would only look guiltier.

"You were saying?" she asked.

The amusement lingered on his lips, which did not ease her discomfort level in the least. How had she let herself get caught staring at him? She'd become an expert at covert crush tactics.

"I was saying that I've been waiting for you to return to the school so I could talk to you about Cassidy. It's not something I felt comfortable discussing via email."

Whatever embarrassment she'd felt just a minute ago

evaporated as Leslie's stomach tanked. "What's going on with Cass? Is something wrong?"

"No, no, no." He put both hands up. "It's nothing to get too alarmed about. I don't have to tell you that Cassidy is one of my standout students. You've seen her in action on the days you've volunteered."

Leslie eased back in her seat, the knot that had instantly formed in her stomach unfurling. "What I've seen is that she turns into a show-off when I'm here."

"That is true." He chuckled. "But in a good way. Her enthusiasm is exactly what I want to see from my students. She comes up with the most thought-provoking questions during class discussions. I was surprised when the third-grade teacher told me that Cassidy barely said a word last year."

"Cass has been slowly coming out of her shell," Leslie said. "I'm not sure if you've noticed the faint marking on her arm, but she used to have a rather large birthmark on her arm and back that made her very self-conscious. She's been undergoing treatment to get it removed."

Her daughter had inherited the port-wine-stain birthmark from Braylon, who'd had a similarly large marking on the side of his face. Cassidy's birthmark had been a contentious subject that nearly drove a wedge between Leslie and Shayla last year after Shayla had spoken to Cass about having it removed without consulting Leslie first.

Leslie had been against it, fearing that her daughter was getting rid of one of the biggest reminders of her father. She had not considered how embarrassment over the birthmark had been holding Cassidy back. Since she'd started treatments to have it removed, Cass had blossomed, going from a child who barely spoke to one who now came home with reprimanding notes from teachers for talking too much in class. The turnaround had been remarkable.

"And here I thought it had something to do with my stellar teaching skills," Gabriel said.

She grinned at his joke. One thing she'd learned in these months since Gabriel Franklin arrived at GEMS was that he was the complete opposite of arrogant. Leslie figured that played into the infatuation, as well. She'd never been one for giant egos.

"You've certainly made an impact on her," she said. She folded her hands on the desk. "I don't know if you realize just how much Cassidy enjoys your class, Mr. Franklin. Not a day goes by that she doesn't have something to say about a science fact she's learned or an experiment you performed. It's a relief to see her so excited about school. She wasn't always this way."

Genuine gratitude cloaked his features. "You have no idea what it means to me to hear that," he said.

He stood and smoothed his hands down the sides of his khaki pants. Now all she could think about was last night's discussion of how cute his butt looked in them.

"Thank you for taking such an interest in our children," she said, reminding herself of why she was here. "And for working so hard to make learning enjoyable."

He shrugged, that humility once again on display. "The more interesting you keep it, the better the students will retain it. At least that's my philosophy."

"It's a good philosophy," she said with a gentle smile. "It's working."

She became acutely aware of the quickening of her pulse as his steady gaze found a home on her mouth and remained there. The faint makings of a grin edged up the corner of his lips once again, and Leslie had to glance away to catch her breath.

Okay. So this turn of events was a bit unsettling.

It had been a while since she'd had a safe crush, but she was certain one of the tenets was that the safe crush should not become privy to her feelings. Gabriel Franklin's knowing smile and penetrating stare indicated that he was all kinds of privy to what she was feeling right now. This could not be good.

"How about that new microscope?" Leslie pointed over her shoulder toward the back of the classroom.

"Yes. It's nice," he said, slipping his hands into his pockets and leaning a hip against the desk.

"You promised you would show it to me," she said.

That didn't sound nearly as innocent coming out of her mouth as it had when she'd said it in her head.

And now he was blushing, too.

Oh, God, could I be more mortified?

"The microscope," Leslie prompted. "You promised you'd show me the new microscope."

Several beats pulsed by as he continued to stare at her, his gaze tracing over her face. Finally, he said, "I did, didn't I?"

He pushed away from the desk and headed for the rear of the classroom. Leslie sucked in a steadying breath before following him.

"I really appreciate the cookies you donated for the bake sale," Mr. Franklin called over his shoulder. "Between the money that raised and the donation from the PTO, I was able to purchase the microscope months earlier than I thought I would be able to. It's been a great addition to the classroom. The students love it."

He'd already fixed a slide in place by the time Leslie arrived at the piece of equipment.

"This is water that I scooped up from Ponderosa Pond." He motioned for her to look into the eyepiece, his eyes brightening with the enthusiasm she so often witnessed when she volunteered in his class. He was such a science geek. Lord, help her, but it only enhanced his sexiness.

"Don't expect Cassidy to go swimming in it anytime soon," he added with a chuckle. "All the kids were horrified."

Leslie lowered her right eye to the eyepiece and grimaced. "I don't blame them. I don't swim, but if I did I wouldn't swim in there, either."

"Why don't you swim?" he asked.

She looked up and realized just how close he was standing to her. Only inches separated them.

Breathe, girl.

She shook her head. "I just…don't like it. I grew up in the city. I never learned how to swim."

"You should learn." Had his voice dropped an octave? "You might find that you enjoy it."

Yes. Yes, it had.

Standing this close, her eyes were drawn back to the attractive way his upper lip dipped in the center. Leslie ordered herself to look away, but then his tongue swept out, glided over his lips, and looking away became next to impossible. She was momentarily mesmerized by the smooth, glistening skin. When she finally drew her eyes back to his, they no longer bore the trace of humor they'd held the first time he caught her staring. This time his gaze was measured, potent and concentrated directly on her.

"You're standing really close," Leslie said.

He nodded. "I realize that."

"Mr. Franklin—"

"You can call me Gabriel, you know," he said, the

pitch of his voice still on the husky side. "We're at school, but technically it's after hours."

Leslie swallowed. Then she swallowed again.

"I...I, uh." She slipped away from the microscope and took several steps back. "I'm not sure that's appropriate."

Appropriate? What was she? Her mother?

Taking yet another step back, Leslie asked, "Can we get back to discussing Cassidy?"

Tilting his head to the side, he rubbed the back of his neck and let out a deep breath. When his gaze returned to her, disappointment was evident in his brown eyes.

"You're right. I apologize if you found anything I said inappropriate, Mrs. Kirkland."

Mrs.

Great. Now she really felt like her mother.

"I didn't mean to—" Leslie started, but he held his hand up, staving off further comment.

"No, you were right. We're here to talk about Cassidy." He expelled another deep breath and continued, "As I was saying earlier, for the most part Cassidy is doing great in class. I do, however, have a couple of issues I wanted to discuss with you." He held up one finger. "Give me just a moment."

Leslie remained at the rear of the classroom while he dashed to the front. She used the brief respite to regain control of her own breathing and to remind herself yet again why it was just plain wrong to nurture any improper feelings toward her daughter's very young science teacher.

A very young science teacher who had asked her to call him by his first name.

Gabriel—Mr. Franklin. *Mr. Franklin*—returned with

a set of manila folders. He flattened one open on the counter.

"As you can see by her quiz scores, Cassidy has definitely grasped the concepts. Her explanations are thorough and well thought out." The prideful smirk that crossed Leslie's lips died a swift death when he continued, "But lately she has displayed an unsettling behavior that is all too common, especially at this age."

"What type of behavior?"

"Cassidy tends to rush through her work so that she can be the first to finish, and she sometimes misses things. Back when I was in school, teachers would reward the kids who finished early, but they don't do that anymore because it's obvious how it can backfire. But many students, especially the competitive ones, still see it as a race."

"Competitive. Yes, well, even though the middle name on her birth certificate is Elizabeth, I think Cass believes it's actually Competition. You should see her on the softball field."

"I can only imagine," he said with a laugh.

His deep chuckle triggered those inappropriate tingles, and suddenly all Leslie could think about was the need to speed up this meeting. She had to put some distance between herself and Gabriel.

Mr. Franklin.

"Cass and I will have a discussion on the importance of taking her time in class," Leslie assured him. "You said you had a couple of issues? What's the second?"

"Homework assignments," he said. "They're not always complete. When I asked Cassidy about it, she said that she tries to get her work done but doesn't always have help."

Shock sent Leslie's brows shooting upward. "I can't

believe she said that. Cassidy knows that I'm there to help her with homework. We're sometimes up until after nine o'clock working on her assignments."

He put both hands up. "You don't have to convince me," he said. "You're one of the most engaged parents I've met since I started teaching here, but you're also a single, working parent. You can't devote all your time to making sure Cassidy does her homework, and you shouldn't have to. She's nine years old. This is the age when she should start becoming accountable for her work." His brow dipped in a frown. "I hope I didn't offend you with that."

"With what?"

"Saying that you're a single, working parent."

Leslie let out a soft laugh. "I *am* a single, working parent," she pointed out. "And while it certainly isn't a walk in the park, it's my job. If Cassidy is having problems completing her assignments, I want to know about it so I can figure out a solution."

"I may have a solution," he said. "Well, not necessarily a solution, but something that can lighten the load." He retrieved another manila folder from the set he'd brought with him. "As one of my best volunteers and the president of the PTO, I want to know what you think about it."

Leslie moved in closer, but made sure not to stand too close. She could not handle the nearness right now.

"I've proposed a new afternoon homework help program in conjunction with Gauthier High School," he began. "The high school students need to earn community service hours, and it would also be a big help to working parents."

"Tutoring?" Leslie asked as she scanned the flyer advertising the program.

"Not exactly," he said. "If the high school student notices that the kid they're trying to help just isn't grasping the information, they can alert the teacher and we can get the student the proper tutoring they need. This program will be strictly homework help. Like I said, it's meant to lighten the load for parents."

"This is a wonderful idea," Leslie said.

"I tried to implement something similar in my previous teaching position, but could never get it off the ground. Now that I'm interim assistant principal I think I have a better shot of making it a reality."

Leslie had been hoping she could avoid talk of the feathers he'd ruffled with some of the changes he'd proposed in his new position, but now that he'd brought it up...

"Speaking of your other role," she began. "As president of GEMS's Parent Teacher Organization, I've been approached by several parents who have concerns over something that they believe is in the wind."

His forehead furrowed. "Is this about the Lock-In?"

"Yes, it is."

His chin fell to his chest and he shook his head. "I don't know how that rumor got started—"

"So it *is* just a rumor?" Leslie questioned. "You don't have plans to cancel or change the Lock-In?"

"Cancel? No. But, yes, I would like to make some changes to it."

Leslie's spine stiffened. She crossed her arms over her chest.

"Mr. Franklin, when parents approached me with this rumor I gave you the benefit of the doubt because I know how quickly facts can get twisted and turned around in this little town. But it seems as if parents had a right to be concerned. Exactly what kind of changes are you proposing?" She held up a finger. "And before you begin, please keep in mind that we've been putting on the Lock-In for years and that it also helped to purchase that microscope you have here."

"Just hear me out," he said, both hands raised in entreaty. "I promise the changes I'd like to make won't hurt the PTO's ability to raise money. In fact, I'm hoping it will help to make even more, all while helping the kids at GEMS prepare for the state test."

"I'm not following," Leslie said.

"As I understand it, in the past the Lock-In has been mainly an all-night party with games and junk food and things like that."

"Yes. And the students love it. They can win prizes and watch movies and hang around with their friends."

"And that's great," he said. "But I think it can be both a fund-raiser and an opportunity for students to learn." He leaned against the counter and folded his arms across his chest. "You've seen me in the classroom, so you know I'm a big believer in making learning fun. In addition to the normal fun and games that usually take place at the Lock-In, I want to gear some of the activities toward learning. We can put on math competitions, hide vocabulary words around the gymnasium and hold a scavenger hunt. I can drag all of my fun science toys in and conduct experiments until the sun comes up. This can be a great way to help students prepare for the end-of-the-year state test."

"Wait." Leslie held up her palm. "Let me get this straight. You never said anything about canceling the Lock-In?"

He shook his head. "Never. Though I have my suspicions about how the rumor was started—"

"I can't reveal my sources," Leslie said.

"I'm not asking you to. However, I am asking for your help in getting the correct information to parents and other members of the PTO. I need parents to be behind me on this. Not just this Lock-In, but on several other ideas I have for the school. Do you think—"

A knock sounded on the door a second before Ardina Scofield's head poked in. "Mr. Frank— Oh, hi, Leslie," she said. "Mr. Franklin, the superintendent of schools is here. Principal Williams asked if you could join them in the cafeteria."

"I'll be right there," Gabriel said. He waited for the secretary to leave before returning his attention to Leslie. "I'm sorry we have to cut this short. I would really like to continue this conversation if you have some time to spare. It's important that the correct information gets out there, and not the rumors that I'm pretty certain the person who just left this room started."

Leslie had to bite her lip to stop herself from making a sound, but she couldn't stop it from twitching.

"You're not betraying your sources," he said. "I know it was Ardina."

"Whoever it was, they apparently got the story wrong."

"Yes, she did. And it's imperative that parents know the truth. Can you help me get the information across to them?"

"Of course," Leslie said.

Relief flooded his face. He reached over and clasped both of her hands between his. "Thank you."

The moment he touched her, tingles started to rain on her skin. He pulled his hand away and ran it up and down his pant leg, but his eyes remained on her. The mixture of confusion and heat in his stare made Leslie question whether her innocent infatuation was one-sided.

But it *had* to be one-sided. He was young and hip and single and just starting out in life. She was a widowed working mother who spent her free time making sure their new puppy didn't leave any smelly surprises on her hardwood floors.

But she wasn't blind, either. She knew that look in Gabriel Franklin's eyes.

This was not one-sided.

"I'll be in touch," he said.

Leslie could only nod.

With one last penetrating look, he turned and left her standing in the room. Leslie slouched against the counter and focused all her energy on pulling in as many deep breaths as she could.

When had her safe crush turned so dangerous?

Gabe fought to remain focused on what Superintendent McCabe was saying, but it would be easier to recite the entire periodic table backward. In his sleep.

He'd lost his ability to comprehend anything the moment Leslie Kirkland entered the school cafeteria. He should be used to his body's reaction to her, but every single time she was near he was shocked at just how much she affected him. He'd had to stop himself from circling her volunteer days on his calendar; but it didn't matter because he had her schedule memorized.

If only he could figure out a way to make her see him as something other than Cassidy's teacher. He had never failed so miserably at getting a woman's attention.

There had been a number of times over the course of the past few months that he'd thought he'd noticed her looking at him with something akin to interest, but maybe it had been wishful thinking on his part. If her reaction to him asking her to call him by his first name wasn't a Mount Olympus–size hint as to how she felt, Gabe didn't know what was.

Leslie Kirkland obviously didn't think of herself as his friend, so he shouldn't think of her that way, either. She was a dedicated volunteer who took a vested interest in her children's education. Period.

She was also gorgeous, sophisticated and—as he'd learned tonight—had the softest hands he'd ever felt.

Gabe tracked her out of the corner of his eye as she walked over to the refreshment table that had been laid out for parents and teachers attending tonight's conference. Her slim figure curved in just the right places, the slight flare of her hips accentuated by her fitted suit jacket. Her rich auburn hair fell in thick waves, reaching just past her shoulders.

And that face—God, that face. Deep-set sable-colored eyes, intoxicatingly smooth light brown skin, lips that haunted his dreams.

This woman had him so twisted inside Gabe could hardly think straight when she was around.

She perused the trays of tiny finger sandwiches and cookies before lifting up a chocolate-chip cookie. His breathing slowed as she brought it to her mouth. Blood started to pound through his veins as her lips parted and—

"Do you agree, Mr. Franklin?"

Gabe snapped to attention.

"Yes," he said.

Wait. What had he just agreed with?

"It was actually Gabriel's idea," John Williams, the school's principal, said. He sent Gabe a questioning look that said he'd better get it together. "We're still figuring out exactly how we're going to schedule it," Mr. Williams continued. "But I think Quiet Time is going to be a big hit with students."

Ah, yes. Quiet Time.

"I predict it will, too," Gabe interjected. "It's something our principal instituted back when I was in high school. For ten minutes each day everyone in the school had to read something. It didn't matter if you were a student, teacher or custodial worker. Even the delivery guy had to stop and read if he happened to come during Quiet Time. There were stations set up throughout the school with books, magazines and newspapers for anyone who didn't have any reading material with them."

"I'm fascinated by this idea," the superintendent said. "It's not too overwhelming. Even nonreaders can concentrate for ten minutes."

"That's the whole idea. And, eventually, they'll learn to enjoy reading a little bit more every day. I went from being a student who hated to read to someone with a paperback-per-week habit, and it's something that has stuck with me to this day."

"Now, that's the kind of habit we want our students to develop," Principal Williams said.

"I haven't gotten to the best part," Gabe continued. "In just a couple of years, the test scores in reading went up over twenty-five percent school-wide."

"A twenty-five-percent increase in just two years? That's all I need to hear," Superintendent McCabe said. "Quiet Time will become a part of the curriculum throughout the entire school system. I'll look into having a committee set this up as soon as possible. You mind working with them?" He directed the question at Gabe.

"Of course I'll work with them," Gabe answered. "You're going to be amazed at the results. Just wait."

"There's Mrs. LeBorde," Principal Williams said. "You need to hear about some of the things she's added to the sixth-grade math course. Gabe, can you meet us in my office in about twenty minutes? Superintendent McCabe has something else to discuss with us."

Gabe told himself that the hint of unease he heard in the principal's voice was just a figment of his imagination.

"Yes. Of course," he said, forcing himself to sound as normal as possible, despite the apprehension sweeping through him.

Had news of the disgruntled parents reached the school board? Were they going to tell him that they were hiring a new permanent assistant principal, someone who hadn't pissed off everyone in the community?

He needed to get control over that rumor about the Lock-In as quickly as possible. This interim assistant principal position was a major stepping-stone on the journey to completing his ultimate goal, and he would be damned if he allowed some false rumor to kill it. He'd worked too hard for this.

Gabe turned and spotted the woman who could be the potential key to putting him back in the parents' good graces.

Leslie stood in front of the table covered with pamphlets highlighting upcoming summer programs. She was chatting with a couple of other parents. For a moment he considered approaching them, but then thought better of it. They had not agreed on just how much she was willing to help him clear up that rumor. He didn't want to pressure her into defending him if she still had lingering doubts about it.

But then she looked directly at him and gave him a slight nod.

That was all the encouragement Gabe needed. He strode up to the group and greeted them with a smile.

"Good evening," he said. "I hope you all don't mind me intruding. I know most of you, but wanted to introduce myself to those of you I haven't met yet. I'm Gabriel Franklin, science teacher and interim assistant principal."

If the parents in this group had heard the rumors floating around about the Lock-In, they didn't let on. They spent several minutes discussing different events that would be held throughout the remaining six weeks of the spring semester, and Gabe even received verbal commitments from several of them to sign up as volunteers. Some of the anxiety that had plagued him since Tristan had told him about the rumors began to dissipate.

Kyle Dorsey, the only male parent in the group, and a mechanical engineer who Gabe had just convinced to come talk to his fifth-grade science class, pointed out that it was after eight o'clock, which meant Parent/Teacher Conference night was officially over. They all bade each other farewell, but before she could leave, Gabe caught Leslie by the hand.

The spark that shot between them rendered him momentarily speechless.

She had to be interested. *Had* to be. Energy like this just didn't exist between two people for no reason.

Her gaze dropped to where he held her hand and then traveled back up to his eyes. Something told Gabe to let go, but he ignored it. Letting go of her amazingly soft hand was the last thing he wanted to do right now.

Unfortunately, she took the choice out of his hands. Literally.

She slowly extricated her delicate fingers from his hold and took a step back.

Slipping his hands into his pockets, Gabe said, "I wanted to thank you for whatever you said to the parents before I came over. I didn't expect that to go so smoothly."

"Actually, I didn't have to say anything. The rumor doesn't seem to be as widespread as you first thought."

"That's a relief."

"However, it *is* still out there, and some *do* believe it."

"Yes, I know," he said, running an aggravated hand through his hair. "Which is why I still need to figure out a way to clear it up. I'm hoping we can set up a meeting with the PTO. It's obvious that I've gotten off on the wrong foot with some of the parents, and I want to rectify that as soon as possible. I *need* to rectify it. It will be very difficult to do my job if the parents aren't behind me."

"I can put you on the agenda at the next PTO meeting," she said. "We meet on the third Wednesday of the month."

Gabe winced. "That's still a couple of weeks away. Look, I know I'm new to Gauthier, but I've been here long enough to recognize the potential damage this rumor can cause if it gets out of hand. I need to nip this issue in the bud, and the sooner the better."

"Oh, believe me, I know," she said. "Of course, you could clear the air instantly by just sending an email through GEMS Connect."

He shook his head. Gabe had considered the school-wide email system used to communicate between parents and faculty, but using it in this instance would be too impersonal.

"This is something that needs to be handled face-to-face. Email leaves too much up for interpretation. I also want to bounce some of my ideas off parents so that they'll know I want their involvement. Please, Les... Mrs. Kirkland."

Her brow rose at his slip, but she didn't comment. Maybe there was hope for them eventually working their way to a first-name basis after all.

"I really need your help with this," Gabe continued. "You're the PTO president. Parents trust you. I've explained my motives to you. You know now that I never had any plans to disrupt the way things are done here. Please help me to get the parents on my side."

She stared at him with a thoughtfulness that made it seem as though she knew her decision could very well affect his entire future. And it could. If the higher-ups in the main school-board office thought he was alienating parents, they wouldn't hesitate to pull this interim-assistant principal position right from under him.

"I'll send an email to the other officers on the PTO board tonight and see what day would work," she said.

Gabe's shoulders sunk with gratitude. "Thank you."

He reached for her hand but pulled back. He was still feeling the effects touching her soft skin had caused during their encounter in his classroom. He didn't want to invite the kind of reaction touching her again could possibly evoke.

Yet, Gabe couldn't stop himself from staring at her, even though he knew she might deem it inappropriate while they stood in the middle of the school cafeteria, surrounded by at least a dozen parents and school staff members still lingering.

He *should* stop, but he couldn't. Not even if his life had depended on it.

There was a warmth to her, a light that radiated from her compelling eyes. It pulled him in, made it impossible to do anything but look into their rich brown depths. He just could not look away.

Finally—*thankfully*—she did it for him.

She glanced toward the door. "I'll be in touch," she said.

"Great," Gabe replied.

Don't say it.

"I'll be waiting."

Dammit. He'd said it.

Gabe braced himself for her reprimand. He experienced a mixture of confusion and encouragement when it didn't come. Was she softening toward him? Had she finally decided that he was an actual person and not just her daughter's teacher?

Should he go for broke and ask her out?

"Good night, Mr. Franklin," she said. And, as if she sensed what he was on the verge of doing, she quickly turned and walked out of the cafeteria.

Gabe ordered himself to look away, but it didn't work. He just continued his inappropriate staring for several moments after she had exited the cafeteria.

Once the school had been emptied of parents and faculty members, Gabe found himself in Mr. Williams's office, sitting in a tweed chair that he would bet was as old as he was. Principal Williams occupied the matching chair opposite his, while Superintendent McCabe perched on the edge of the desk, a clear assertion of his position of authority.

Gabe tried to read the body language of both men, but he was getting nothing. Of course, he'd never been demoted before, so he wasn't sure what signs he should look for.

The superintendent leaned forward and clasped his fingers together.

"It's pretty late, so why don't we just get to it," he said. "Now, what I'm about to share with the two of you is strictly off-the-record until the official announcement is made, but since it affects your schools—and careers—I thought you should know about it."

Gabe held his breath, preparing himself for the blow.

"I'm sure you both have seen the progress that's been made on the new high school being built on that land the school board purchased on Highway 421 between Gauthier and Maplesville."

That was not exactly how Gabe had expected this conversation to start, but anything that didn't begin with *we've hired a new assistant principal* was okay with him.

"The facility is one of the most advanced designs in the country," McCabe continued. "Eighty percent of the school will run on solar energy, there's an on-site water-treatment plant and the technology in the classrooms will blow your minds. We already have school administrators from around the country asking for permission to tour it."

"What does this have to do with GEMS, Patrick?" Principal Williams asked.

"This is the exciting part." The superintendent rubbed his palms together. Such drama. "I was approached by the Department of Education about a program they want to test. They would like Maplesville's and GEMS's middle-school students to be a part of the pilot study. The plan would combine the middle schools in Maplesville and Gauthier into one state-of-the-art campus."

"What about the elementary-school students?" Williams asked.

"They would remain here."

"They want to break up GEMS?" Gabe asked.

Williams straightened in his chair. "The elementary and middle schools have always been together."

"That's because the student population has never been large enough to justify having a separate elementary and middle school," Superintendent McCabe said. "But if the student body is combined with that of Maplesville Middle School, we would have over six hundred students. The campus is currently designed to accommodate just over eight hundred, and it sits on enough acreage that there's room for growth for years to come. This is a golden opportunity, John," McCabe said. "This school would be a model for schools around the country."

Gabe was still trying to figure out how this affected him. "What grades would attend the middle school?" he asked.

"Sixth, seventh and eighth grades."

"Our eighth graders go to the high school," Williams pointed out. "You know how the kids are here, Patrick. They look forward to attending high school in eighth grade. It's one of the things that makes Gauthier unique."

"Again, it's because of the low student-body count. We could combine both schools in Gauthier and make it a K-through-twelfth-grade campus and there still wouldn't be enough students to fill an entire school. It's a miracle we're able to keep them both open."

"Don't start that," Principal Williams said.

"I know, I know." The superintendent raised his hands. "Don't worry. The schools in Gauthier are safe."

Safe? What were they talking about?

"A merger will be a hard sell to the community," Williams said. "And, technically, that campus is within Maplesville city limits. You know darn well how the people around here will react to that."

"John, we cannot allow small-town politics to get in the way of this. If we agree to take part in this pilot program, it would mean more federal dollars into this school system than we've seen in the twenty years I've been a part of it. And it's not just the school system's bank account that would benefit. This is good news for both of you, too."

Finally.

School politics had never interested him, although Gabe knew eventually he would have to play the game if he was going to make it in school administration. Right now he didn't care about the politics behind this new merger; he was more concerned with how it would affect his career.

"John, you're number one in line for taking over as principal at the new merged school," the superintendent said. "You have seniority, and I think you're better equipped to handle a school of that size. Shelia Melancon would move over from her assistant principal position at Maplesville Middle."

"What about Grayson?" Principal Williams asked of the principal at Maplesville Middle School. "Where does he fit in?"

Gabe had yet to hear his name mentioned. He was more worried about where *he* would fit in.

"Grayson will move into your position here." The superintendent turned to Gabe. "Mr. Franklin, with all the personnel swaps that would have to take place, the school board has decided that bringing in someone from outside of the school system to take over the assistant principal position here at GEMS would just disrupt things. It makes more sense to have you take over the position permanently."

Excitement began to pump through Gabe's bloodstream like a locomotive on speed.

"That…ah…that would be fantastic," he said.

"Even though you've been here less than a year, you would still have seniority over whomever we bring in," the superintendent continued. "You have the academic credentials, *and* you already have a relationship with the community, which is vitally important."

Gabe had never been one to hyperventilate, but for the first time in his life he felt close to it. He surreptitiously sucked in a couple of deep breaths and told himself to calm down.

But how in the hell was he supposed to remain calm? He had so much riding on this it kept him awake at night.

Being in a position to bring about change in the education system was important to him, but two main driving forces had been behind his decision to go back to graduate school and get his master's in school administration: making his high school science teacher, Mr. Caldwell, proud and making enough money to help his family back in Houston.

Gabe hated to be all about the dollar, but with the increase in his salary he would be able to help his baby sister, Daniela, as she entered college in the fall and he would be able to send his baby brother, Elias, to private school for his final two years of high school. Getting Elias away from his current high school was at the top of Gabe's priority list. He didn't want his brother wandering down the path he'd been on at that age. Elias didn't have someone like Mr. Caldwell to save him from himself the way Gabe had.

"How soon would all this happen?" Gabe asked, hoping he didn't sound too eager.

"You would officially take over as assistant principal at the end of this school year."

Yes. That was less than two months away. It meant his new salary would kick in around that time, too.

"There's just one thing," Superintendent McCabe said. "The residents of both Gauthier and Maplesville have to approve of the merger. School-board elections are in less than four weeks, and there's not a single member of the board who will support the merger if residents are against it." He looked from Gabe to Principal Williams. "I'm counting on the two of you to rally the support of the parents here at GEMS. You must get them on board with this if we're going to go forward."

Dammit. Gabe knew it was too good to be true.

Half the parents at GEMS still didn't know him and the other half didn't trust him because of the rumor Ardina had started about the Lock-In. How in the hell was he going to convince them to support *anything* he advocated for?

Gabe's eyes fell shut as he blew out a deep breath. Now more than ever he would need Leslie Kirkland's help to get him back in the good graces of the parents in Gauthier.

Chapter 4

"Cassidy, you have exactly one minute to get out of that bathroom," Leslie called from her own bathroom. "The school bus will be here any minute."

"I'm almost done."

Leslie pitched her head back and sighed at the ceiling. The child was only nine years old. *Nine.* And already she was a bathroom hog. How was she going to handle the teen years? Leslie had considered adding on a third bathroom in a few years, but she wasn't sure she would be able to wait that long.

Leslie stopped in the middle of putting on her eyeliner.

If she followed through with the plans that had been floating around in her head, they wouldn't be in this house by the time Cassidy became a teenager. They wouldn't be here by the time she reached age ten.

Leslie tried to ignore the nauseating sensation that

began to swirl in her stomach as she threw on a touch of mascara and swiped gloss over her lips.

When she arrived in the kitchen, Cassidy and Kristi were slipping on their backpacks.

"Have you two checked to make sure Buster didn't have an accident?"

They nodded in unison.

"You looked in all of her usual places?"

Cassidy ticked the list off on her fingers. "At the end of the hallway, in the corner in the living room and in Kristi's room."

"Under the coffee table?" Leslie asked.

"Yes," Kristi said with a firm nod. "No accidents. Buster is becoming a big girl."

"With a stupid name," Cassidy said. She stuck her tongue out at Kristi when the five-year-old protested.

Leslie would never tell Kristi that the name she'd chosen for the dog—which was purchased on her birthday, thus giving her naming privileges—was stupid. However, she could think of a million more appropriate names for a female Yorkshire terrier with pink ribbons at her ears.

The screech of the school bus's tires set them all into motion.

"Okay, okay, get going," Leslie said, ushering the girls out of the house. She gave them both pecks on the cheeks and stood on the porch steps to watch them board the bus. She waited until it made a right on Oak Street before going back into the house to grab her laptop.

The time it took to deal with Kristi's tantrum over Cassidy using the strawberry-scented lotion that Shayla had given her for a birthday present had stolen any chance Leslie had of sitting at the table for a nice breakfast. She would have to find something she could eat on the road.

Just as she was pressing the button on the single-serve coffeemaker, Leslie caught a whiff of a foul but familiar odor.

"Dammit, Buster! You *would* wait until the girls were gone, wouldn't you?"

The puppy, which was currently dancing around her feet, let out a squeaky bark.

Leslie followed her nose to the pile of dog poop in the arched entryway that led from the kitchen to the rarely used formal dining room.

"Looks as if you've got a new favorite spot."

She cursed under her breath as she returned to the kitchen for paper towels. One of the contingencies for getting a dog was that the girls were supposed to be responsible for cleaning up after her. Leslie was convinced they had made some sort of pact with Buster. The dog never made a mess when Cassidy and Kristi were around.

Just to rub salt in the wound, Buster followed after her, yapping and jumping up and down at her legs, as if taunting her. Leslie gave her the meanest stare she could muster.

"I'm not a violent person, but sometimes I really want to strangle you."

The dog yapped again and then started to pant, her tongue hanging out in the most adorable way. Leslie exhaled a tired laugh. It was either that or choke the little fur ball.

After cleaning up the mess and scrubbing her hands like a surgeon before surgery, Leslie grabbed a granola bar from the healthy-snack basket she kept on the counter and her travel mug from the coffeemaker.

Buster's accident had put her another ten minutes behind, but at least the early risers who worked at the local concrete factory and oil refineries had made their way out of Gauthier by the time she got on the road. Her smooth sailing came to a screeching halt when she hit the tiny town of Talisheek and encountered a wall of traffic.

Leslie's head fell back against the headrest. She'd forgotten about the restriping work that started today. It was scheduled to last two weeks.

"Reason number one hundred and twelve to move to Houston."

She'd grown so weary of the forty-minute commute into Slidell—forty minutes if she didn't get stuck behind a slow-moving vehicle along the twenty-mile stretch of one-lane-only highway, that was. Thank goodness for her boss and his giant, understanding heart. After a decade of getting caught behind school busses with a dozen stops or tractor trailers hauling sugarcane during harvest season, Stewart Campbell no longer batted an eye when she walked into the office a half hour late.

But she was tired of handing Stew excuses. And she was tired of this long, solitary drive that gave her too much time to think. Too much time to reminisce about the life she'd once led, to contemplate a future that was no longer possible.

A familiar pain tightened Leslie's chest.

Never again would she witness the joy on her daughters' faces when they hugged their dad after a year-long deployment. Never again would she rest in Braylon's arms while they swung lazily on the porch swing and made plans for the day he reached his twenty years with the Army and was able to retire.

This frustratingly long drive gave her too much damn time to remember. Remembering hurt too much.

Leslie swallowed the lump of emotion bottlenecking in her throat and blew out a deep breath.

She needed to meet with Stew. It was time she broached the subject of transferring to the office in The Woodlands, a suburb due north of Houston. She'd debated it back and forth for months, weighed the pros and cons.

The cons were winning by a landslide.

Aside from the upheaval that came with any major move, Leslie also knew that uprooting the girls right now would be hard on them emotionally. They were both enjoying school and their friends. Cass loved being one of the best players on her softball team, and Kristi had joined the Diamond Dolls, the adorable cheerleading squad at GEMS.

But Leslie knew the hardest thing for the girls to endure would be leaving their aunt Shayla.

Shayla had lived on the West Coast for two decades, seeing the girls only a couple of times before moving back to Gauthier after Braylon's death. Since her return she had become an integral part of their family. It wasn't just Shayla; Xavier had slipped so effortlessly into the role of being the male figure in the girls' lives. The thought of taking Kristi and Cass away from two people who had come to mean so much to them made Leslie's stomach hurt.

But it was more than just her girls' love for their aunt and uncle tying her to Gauthier. She couldn't just pack up and leave during her term as president of the PTO, could she? And what about church? She'd been a member of the choir for eight years and had served on the finance board for three.

Even Buster had climbed onto the list of cons. The puppy was just starting to acclimate herself. Who knew what moving to a new house would do to her.

Yet, despite the horde of items crowding the con side of the list, there was one thing on the pro side that outweighed everything else. If she left Gauthier, then maybe she could finally, *finally* put these memories of Braylon behind her and move on with her life.

Leslie knew she could not continue living this way. The memories were like quicksand, slowly pulling her down, keeping her in this mental space she no longer wanted to occupy.

"Which is why you have to leave."

She turned up the volume on the radio and sang along to the gospel CD she kept in case of emotional emergencies.

When she finally arrived at the office, she felt marginally in control of her emotions. She got out of the car and headed straight for Stewart Campbell's office, the determination to finally make this move pushing her feet forward.

"Where's Stew?" Leslie asked when she walked into the darkened office.

"He had to fly to New York this morning for an emergency meeting at headquarters," Kianna Sims, her boss's executive assistant, said as she breezed into the office and set a collection of files on it.

Leslie couldn't deny the relief that washed over her at the reprieve from asking for the transfer. She was *such* a coward.

"Why the urgency?" she asked Kianna.

The executive assistant shrugged. "Don't know, but the quarterly report is due to be released next week."

Leslie grimaced. They all knew that an emergency

trip to headquarters so close to a report release didn't spell good news.

With Stewart gone, Leslie was the most senior employee in the office and technically in charge, but in this office, which ran like a well-oiled machine, it didn't really matter.

She'd joined the financial capitalist firm as an analyst shortly after she and Braylon were married, and in that time she and her coworkers had become a family.

The office was located in Slidell, but most of their clients were based in downtown New Orleans, requiring multiple analysts to make the hour-long drive several times a week. Everyone in the office had agreed that, as the only single mother in the group, Leslie should be exempt from making the trek into the city just in case her girls had an emergency at school that required her to return quickly to Gauthier.

She loved these people. They had seen her through two pregnancies and helped her through the death of her husband. Leslie could not begin to comprehend how much she would miss them if she transferred to Houston.

When. When she transferred to Houston. She'd already made the decision to leave. But if she could, she would take them all with her.

The morning coasted by without incident. After lunch, Leslie and two of her coworkers sat in on a conference call with Stewart. To everyone's relief the news out of New York wasn't bad at all. In fact, it was fabulous. The firm had exceeded expected profits for the quarter. There was so much patting on the back that Leslie figured they would all have bruises by the end of the day.

As they filed out of the conference room, she grabbed

a cup of tea from the break room before returning to her desk to tackle the emails that had sprouted and multiplied during the past hour. An email from the GEMS Connect system caught her eye. She should have been ashamed of the excited tingles that erupted throughout her belly when she spotted Gabriel Franklin's name in the sender section, but she was too busy darting for her computer mouse to feel shame.

Mrs. Kirkland,

It was a true pleasure seeing you at this past Tuesday's Parent/Teacher Conference night. I wanted to thank you again for being such a supportive and engaged parent. You make a difference not just in Cassidy's education, but in the academic lives of all GEMS students, who benefit from your involvement in the school.

I'm writing in hopes that we can meet to discuss the agenda for the special PTO meeting we talked about on Tuesday. It is imperative that parents get the full story regarding my changes to the Lock-In event. Would you be willing to have coffee with me this evening so that we can discuss?

Sincerely,

Gabriel

Leslie stared at the screen for several moments, unsure how she should respond.

Coffee? He'd asked her out for coffee? And look at the way he'd signed it. *Gabriel.* No Mr. Franklin. No GEMS Interim Assistant Principal. Just Gabriel.

"Leslie?"

Leslie's head popped up. Kianna stood in her open doorway, a sheaf of papers in her hands.

"You needed something?" She minimized the email on her computer screen.

"Stewart asked if you could sign off on these security statements."

"Has he read them?"

"Yes. They just need a signature."

Leslie motioned for her to bring the papers to her and signed the flagged pages. Then she began to pack up her work to take home with her.

"I have to meet with the assistant principal at the girls' school, so I'll be leaving a little early today," she told Kianna.

"Uh-oh. Who's in trouble, Cassidy or Kristi?"

"No, no, no. It's nothing like that," Leslie said with a laugh. At least the girls weren't in trouble. She, on the other hand, had better control these pesky little tingles that kept going off in her stomach before she found *herself* in trouble.

Once Kianna left, Leslie pulled up the email again and went through a mental list of why it would be a bad idea—a stupid, horrible, ridiculously terrible idea—to have coffee with Gabriel Franklin. Even when coffee was just coffee, there was always the risk of someone seeing it as something more than *just* coffee. What if someone saw them together and took it as something more than what it was meant to be? What if Gabriel *meant* for it to be something more?

They had chemistry. There was no way to deny it. Leslie had run out of benign explanations for the palpable attraction that had soared between them Tuesday night. There had been only one other time in her life when she'd connected with another person so immediately, so intimately. And it scared the hell out of her to think of connecting with someone else on that level again.

Leslie rolled her eyes. "It's just coffee, for crying out loud."

Yet, when she replied to his email, she suggested they meet in his office at the school. Because she really was the biggest coward on the face of the planet.

She quickly packed up her briefcase and asked Kianna to send an office-wide text for anyone to contact her via her cell if they needed her.

The girls were both going over to The Jazzy Bean after school today, per Shayla's request. She was trying new healthy bakery recipes and wanted to use the girls as guinea pigs, a role both Cassidy and Kristi relished. Leslie was just happy that she didn't have to pay a babysitter.

Less than an hour later, she pulled into the visitors' parking lot at the school just as the last yellow bus was turning onto the highway. She entered through glass double doors and headed for the front office. Ardina Scofield stood at the copier, catching papers as they shot out of the machine.

Leslie rapped her knuckles on the counter to get her attention. "Hi, Ardina."

"Hey," she answered, then turned her attention back to the copy machine.

"I'm here to see Mr. Franklin," Leslie provided.

"Yeah, he told me you were coming. He's in there." The secretary nudged her chin toward the assistant principal's office.

Okay. That was awkward.

With a confused shake of her head, Leslie walked in the direction Ardina had directed her. She found

Gabriel sitting behind a large wooden desk, his head bowed over a stack of file folders.

"Mr. Franklin?"

He looked up and a broad smile flashed across his face. "Mrs. Kirkland." He rose from behind the desk and came around to meet her. "Thank you for coming on such short notice," he said.

He gestured to one of the seats directly in front of the desk. Then, instead of returning to his chair, he sat in the seat opposite her, putting his knee in such close proximity to her leg that Leslie could feel his body heat.

Lord, let this meeting be a quick one. It was getting harder for her to control her feelings for her not-so-safe-anymore crush.

"I hope my asking you here didn't disrupt your evening routine too much," he started.

"Not at all," Leslie replied. "My girls are with their aunt at her coffee shop."

"That's the place on Main Street, right? It's a nice hangout, especially on a Friday night when there's jazz and dancing."

"I've only been there once on a Friday night."

"No way." He looked at her as if she must be joking.

Leslie nodded and shrugged. "My sister-in-law is always hounding me to come to jazz night. She's even offered to pay for the babysitter."

"You should. The music acts are impressive, especially for a town as small as Gauthier." He paused for a moment, then, in a low voice edged with warmth, said, "Maybe I'll see you there one Friday. Maybe this Friday, if you're not busy?"

Leslie's eyes flew to his. Had he just asked her out?

"This Friday?"

What if by *Maybe I'll see you there?* he literally

meant that maybe he would see her there and just wave. As in *Hi, Mrs. Kirkland. Nice to see you here*.

But what if he *had* just asked her out? What if her daughter's very young, very handsome science teacher had just asked her out on a date?

"You seem to be thinking *really* hard," he said.

His invitation—if that was indeed what it had been— had caught her off guard. Leslie had been asked out on a number of dates this past year, but never by someone to whom she was wildly attracted.

"Mrs. Kirkland?"

"Yes," she said much too loudly. "I am thinking… about the PTO meeting. What exactly do you want us to discuss?"

The low timber of his deep chuckle sent ripples across her skin. He shook his head and said, "You're not going to make this easy for me, are you?"

The look in his eyes took away any doubt that his words a few minutes ago had been anything but an invitation to join him on Friday. He had asked her out. He was interested. So was she. At least she was more interested in him than any other man she had come in contact with in the past two years.

But, God, was she ready to take this next step? Were her children ready? How would this town react to her stepping out with a man on her arm—a much younger man?

She couldn't deal with this. Not right now.

"The meeting, Mr. Franklin?"

His steady gaze bore into hers for several moments before he nodded slightly and said in a resigned voice, "Yes, the meeting."

Leslie's entire body relaxed with the relief that he would not push her any further or come right out and ask her on a date. She needed time to unpack this, spread it out in her mind and decide whether or not she was truly ready to embark on this next part of her life.

Gabriel clasped his hands between his parted knees and began, "It occurred to me during Parent/Teacher Conference night that even though I had a pseudo-introduction to parents when I came on board as the new science teacher, that was mostly to the parents of the students I personally teach.

"As the interim assistant principal, I need to become a familiar face to *all* parents. With this special PTO meeting I can kill two birds with one stone—clear up the false rumors about wanting to cancel the Lock-In and make a formal introduction to all the parents who don't know me. I really need to get the parents on my side," he finished.

"If you want to get the parents of GEMS on your side, it's very simple," Leslie said. She leaned in. "I'll tell you the secret."

Gabe's head dropped into his hands.

"That is not what I wanted to hear."

"Probably not, but it's the truth," Leslie said. She sat back in her chair, crossed her legs and folded her hands over her knee. "If you want the parents around here on your side, your best bet is to leave everything exactly the way it is. To say this town is resistant to change is an understatement."

"*Change* isn't a dirty word, especially when it comes to education," Gabe stated. "There are so many new and innovative ideas out there. Technology is changing by the second, and if GEMS doesn't change with it, it's going to get left behind."

"You're preaching to the choir, Mr. Franklin. And

it's possible that if the right person delivered the message some parents may get on board, but I'm not sure you're the right person to deliver it."

"It's because I'm new, isn't it?" She didn't answer, but Gabe could tell just by her expression that he was onto something. "I knew it." He shook his head. "When I accepted this position, I told Mr. Williams that people would take exception to it. Hell, I don't blame them. Here I am, brand-new, and I'm now in a position of authority over teachers who have been here for years."

"It is a difficult position to be in, isn't it?"

The look of understanding that stole over her face, combined with the empathetic lilt in her voice, brought Gabe more comfort than he would have expected. He hadn't realized just how much he needed an ally, how alone he'd felt in all of this.

One of the reasons he'd fallen in love with this town was because, at first, the town had fallen in love with him. He'd fit in from the very beginning, which was why it had been such a jolt to his system when he'd learned that he was at the top of everyone's shit list because of the rumors Ardina had started. Just like that, the love affair was over. The stark reminder that he was an outsider had never hit home more than it had this week.

"I can't change that I'm new in town," Gabe said. "But I'm here now, and I am in the position to make what I believe are positive changes to the education system. How do you suggest I go about getting parents on board with this?"

"The first would be an apology." She held up a hand before he had the chance to protest. "It doesn't matter whether you think you have anything to apologize for. An apology will go a long way in soothing hurt feelings. Second, you must explain that you never had any intentions of cancelling the Lock-In."

"I didn't, so that's not a problem."

"Also, let them know that you want them to be engaged. Ask for their input."

"Which is exactly what I want," Gabe said. "This isn't a dictatorship. I don't want anyone to think I'm just stepping in and trying to rule the day."

"That's good to know," Leslie said. "And that's what you need to make sure parents understand. Just be honest and open with them. The people here may be resistant to change, but once they recognize that the changes you're suggesting will help further their children's education, they will rally behind you like nothing you've ever seen. We all just want what's best for our kids."

Gabe felt a slight brush of guilt. He wasn't being totally honest with her right now, but Superintendent McCabe had stressed that news of the potential merger was to be kept under wraps.

"I also think when you explain the changes you want to make to the Lock-In parents will climb on board. It really is…" She paused in the middle of her sentence and pointed to his purple windbreaker. "Jefferson Davis Panthers? In Near Northside?"

"Yeah," Gabe said. "It's my alma mater."

A smile broke out over her lovely face. "Is your butt still sore from all the whippings you used to take from the James Madison Marlins?"

"No way?" He laughed. "You went to Madison? What year?"

She looked at him as if he'd lost every single bit of his good sense. "As if I would tell you."

"Why not?"

She just continued to stare at him with that look of

half horror, half incredulousness. And just like that everything became crystal clear.

"That's what this is about, isn't it? You think I'm too young for you." He leaned forward in his seat and, holding her steady gaze, said, "I'm not much younger than you are, Leslie."

Her name slipped off his tongue so easily that Gabe didn't have a chance to rein it back. He waited for her to protest, but she didn't. She studied him, her eyes never leaving his face. Finally, she said, "You're young enough. I'm not ancient, but I'm pretty sure we were born in different decades."

"Two people can be born a day apart and still be born in different decades. Try again."

"What do you think I'm trying to do?"

"The way I see it, you're trying to use our age difference as a reason to ignore the many attempts I've made to get to know you better," he said.

"Many?"

"I've been trying for months," he said. "I thought I'd lost my edge, but it's not me. It's you. Why are you playing so hard to get?"

Her head reared back slightly, and that look of confusion in her eyes turned to one of awed understanding. "I was right. In your earlier email when you asked me out for coffee, you meant *coffee* coffee."

"What exactly is *coffee* coffee?"

"You know what I mean," Leslie said. "There's a difference between just going out for coffee and going out for *coffee* coffee."

"Ah. Okay, I think I get it now," Gabe said. "In that case the answer is yes. I did mean to ask you out for *coffee* coffee. And when I mentioned catching a show at The Jazzy Bean this Friday night, that was an invitation to *coffee* coffee, too."

She shook her head, her expression once again puzzled. "But why?" she asked.

"Why?"

"Yes, why? I'm a single mother with two school-age girls. I was married for over ten years before my husband died. I spend my free time thinking about buying extra life insurance and finding slow-cooker recipes that freeze well."

"I've got a great paella recipe," Gabe said with a grin. "It was my *abuelita*'s specialty."

She rolled her eyes. "You know what I'm saying. I don't fit in your age demographic."

He leaned back and crossed his arms over his chest. "Exactly how young do you think I am?"

"Too young for me to consider having *coffee* coffee with you," she said.

There was no way he would let her turn him down because of something this insignificant. For one thing, she could not be more than a couple of years older than he was. Though, it was not as if he would care if she *was* older than that. Age didn't mean a damn thing to him. But, apparently, it meant enough to Leslie that she would allow it to get in the way of this chemistry that had been sizzling between them for months.

"I'm twenty-eight years old," Gabe said.

"You're even younger than I thought."

Gabe pitched his head back and groaned. He looked at her again and, with every ounce of what he was feeling bared to her, said, "What is it going to take to make you see me the way I see you?"

"How do you see me?"

"I see you as someone who is smart and sensitive

and passionate about the people you love. You're dedicated and thoughtful, and you give your time and energy without hesitation." Gabe scooted to the edge of his chair, closing the distance between them. His voice lowered, he said, "I'm about to be really inappropriate, but I also see you as someone who is sexy as hell. You were sexy as hell before I knew you were a widowed mother of two little girls, and you were just as sexy after I learned that you were."

He reached over and took her hand in his. "So you're thirty-one years old. Why does that matter?"

"I'm thirty-four."

"So are millions of other people. Still doesn't matter." He gave her hands a gentle but firm squeeze. "I like you, Leslie. For all the reasons I just stated. You're smart and sexy and sensitive and giving and sexy."

Her cheeks reddened. "You said that already."

"It bears repeating." Gabe captured her chin with his fingers and nudged up her face. "Are you ready to stop fighting this and admit that you like me?"

He could see the internal war happening within her as she studied his face and, for a minute, panic gripped his chest at the thought of pushing her so hard that he'd possibly pushed her away. But then she looked up at him and said, "We have to be discreet."

Excitement and relief crashed through him at the same time.

"I can be discreet," Gabe said.

"That means no Friday nights at The Jazzy Bean," she said. "There are too many wagging tongues around, and I'm not ready to give them something else to talk about. Whether or not our ages mean anything to you doesn't matter. It will mean something to the people in this town."

He held up his hands. "Whatever you're comfortable with, Leslie. I can now call you Leslie, right?"

The smile that graced her lips was so mesmerizing Gabe lost the ability to think about anything but eventually tasting them.

"Yes," she said. "You can call me Leslie, Gabriel."

"It's Gabe," he said, returning her smile. "My *mami* and *abuelita* are the only two people who call me Gabriel." He blew out a breath he hadn't realized he'd been holding, suddenly feeling lighter than he had in months. "Now that that's taken care of, why don't you tell me how someone who went to James Madison ended up in this tiny town?"

"I married one of Gauthier's native sons," she answered. "Braylon and I lived on an Army base in North Carolina for a few months, but I moved here permanently once I got pregnant with Cassidy. Braylon didn't want his children growing up as Army brats. How did you hear about Gauthier?"

"Tristan Collins told me about the opening for a science teacher. He and I were college roommates."

"He's pretty popular around here. The high school band has made it to the statewide band competition for the past three years with him at the helm."

"Tristan loves it here, and he knew I was getting burned-out at the school where I taught in New Orleans. I was ready for a slower pace."

"Well, you'll certainly get that here," she said.

"But I like it. Don't you?"

"Gauthier has grown on me, but I have to admit it took a while." She laughed. "At first, it drove me crazy. Coming from Houston—I grew up in Hiram Clarke—I was used to city life. It took me the longest time to get used to falling asleep to the sound of crickets instead of traffic and police sirens." The corners of her mouth dipped in a frown. "Now I can't imagine my girls growing up anyplace else. Gauthier is the only home they've ever known."

"As far as I can tell, it's a great place to raise a family. It's small but people seem to like it that way."

"We do," she said. "Maplesville has grown so quickly over the past few years, and many in Gauthier were afraid that we would have to do the same if we wanted to keep up, but I'm happy the people here have decided not to go the route of Maplesville. Yes, our schools are small, and we don't have any chain restaurants or movie theaters or any of the other modern conveniences most people can't live without, but that's the way we like it around here. It's what makes this place home. It's what makes it special."

Gabe captured her hand again. He gently stroked her smooth skin, desire flooding his bloodstream at the realization that this woman he had been wanting all these months had finally opened herself to the possibility of something real happening between them.

"I had my reasons for liking this town before you walked in this door today," Gabe said. "But Gauthier just became a lot more special to me."

Tugging the bill of her baseball cap down to shield her eyes from the glaring sun, Leslie cupped her hands around her mouth and started to chant, "Go, Cubs, go! Go, Cubs, go!"

She motioned for the crowd to join in as the seven- and eight-year-olds exited the field, making way for the nine- and ten-year-old softball players. She had never been one for loud public displays, that was, until her daughter started playing softball. After Cass's first home run, Leslie had gone from meek spectator to the loudest fan in the stands.

She was also, according to Cassidy, the most annoying fan, especially when she whipped out her trusty bottle of sunscreen.

Leslie grabbed two bottles of SPF 70 from her bag and made her way down the bleachers. She, along with the softball coach, slathered sunscreen on both the home and away teams. She then went over to Kristi and the rest of the Diamond Dolls on the sideline and coated them, too.

When she returned to the bleachers, Shayla was sitting in their usual spot.

"Hey there," Leslie greeted. "Xavier parking the car?"

"He got called into the ER at Maplesville General. The on-call doc decided to take an early-morning fishing trip and was caught in traffic on his way back. Xavier just texted to say he should be here by the third or fourth inning." Shayla pointed to Kristi. "Just look at that little thing in her cheerleader uniform. Is she the most adorable child in the world or what?" She stood and jiggled her hips. "Yay, Kristi! Shake it, baby!"

Kristi turned, slapped an embarrassed hand over her eyes and returned her attention to the baseball diamond.

"Is Cass nervous about the first game of the season?" Shayla asked as she reclaimed her seat.

"She says she isn't, but I found her pacing the hallway this morning with her softball bat. I told her it's just a game and that she's just here to have fun. I don't want her to feel too much pressure to perform."

"Okay, Les, you know I loved my baby brother, but if *he* was the one giving Cassidy that pep talk this morning it would have been the complete opposite of what you said. Braylon would have told her to go out there and kick ass. Hard."

Leslie laughed and nodded. "Yes, he would have. Can you just imagine him out here?"

She'd thought about Braylon more than usual this morning. The moment she'd arrived at the ballpark and had seen all the fathers in the bleachers, Leslie instantly had thought of how much Braylon would have cherished this. He had always been so proud of his girls. She could picture him standing along the fence line, yelling words of encouragement to Cass and her teammates. Or yelling obscenities at the umpire for a bad call. She knew Braylon. He would have been the most obnoxious dad at the ballpark.

Leslie pulled in a steadying breath.

Braylon *was* here. He was watching over them just as he'd promised he would whenever they'd had The Talk. They'd had The Talk a number of times during their marriage. It was part of being a military couple during a time of war. Each time he left on a tour of duty, Braylon would promise that he would always be with her in spirit, even if he wasn't here in physical form.

Leslie's mouth dipped in a frown.

What would Braylon think if he saw her here with someone else? With another man? How would he feel if Gabriel was sitting next to her in the bleachers, yelling encouragement to Cassidy, or standing along the sidelines praising Kristi's cheerleading skills?

In the months since she'd even remotely considered dating again, the one thing that had given her the most pause was the fear of disrespecting Braylon's memory by bringing another man into his daughters' lives. Even though Braylon would have wanted her to move on.

He'd never meant for her to be alone, had never meant for their girls to grow up without a father.

Why hadn't he stuck around to be the husband and father he'd wanted for his family? Why did he have to leave her? Why couldn't she have figured out a way to help him so that he would have stayed with them?

Leslie straightened her spine. She would not allow her mind to go there. She had crossed that stage in her grief, and she would be damned if she returned to questioning Braylon's actions over and over again. He was gone. It was done.

"Hey, are you okay?"

Leslie whipped her gaze to Shayla. "What?"

"Are you okay?" her sister-in-law asked a second time. "You looked…I don't know…spooked."

"I'm fine," Leslie said. She pointed to the baseball field. "Look, Cass is up to bat."

Resolved, Leslie turned her attention to what mattered here and now. She was here to support her children.

She and Shayla both cheered Cassidy on as she struck out in three quick swings. The two batters who followed did the same, and in no time at all the game had gone through three innings. Xavier arrived just as Cassidy was going up to bat again in the fifth inning.

"You got this one, Cass!" Xavier shouted as he slid onto the metal bleachers next to Shayla.

Cassidy looked up into the stands, smiled at Xavier and hit a grounder to third base. The entire crowd went wild. Even those rooting for the opposing team cheered. They had all been waiting so long for *something* to finally happen.

Leslie leaned forward and looked over at her brother-in-law. "She just wanted to show off for you."

"I knew my girl would give her uncle Xavier something to cheer about."

Leslie shook her head and laughed. She could not have asked for a more loving soul to be there as a surrogate father for her daughters. Even before he and Shayla had married, Xavier told her that she could count on him for anything the girls would ever need. Just thinking about the heartfelt conversation made Leslie's chest ache with gratitude. Knowing that she wasn't alone in this, that her family would always be here for her, brought her immeasurable comfort.

A weight settled in her stomach as she thought about what would happen when she told Xavier and Shayla about their impending move to Texas. She had yet to make it official, but as soon as Stewart returned from New York, the ball would be set into motion. The contentment she'd experienced just a moment ago died a swift death at the thought of breaking the news to her family.

The game ended with the Cubs winning two to zero, and as usual, whether win or lose, they all went out for ice cream at Hannah's Ice Cream shop in neighboring Maplesville.

By the time they arrived home, all Leslie wanted to do was shower and crawl under the covers. Instead of heading for the shower, she sat on the edge of her bed. From her nightstand she picked up the framed five-by-seven of Braylon in his dress uniform and stared at her husband's handsome face.

She'd always thought he was incredibly handsome, despite the dark purple port-wine-stain birthmark that stretched across a portion of the right side of his face, behind his ear and down his neck. Her lack of a reaction to his birthmark had been one of the reasons Leslie had figured they'd been meant to be together.

She'd met him at a bar on South Padre Island during spring break her freshmen year at Rice. He and several of his Army buddies had been at the Coast Guard installation there and had come into the bar after a long day of exercises. Leslie, on a dare from one of her girlfriends, had entered a wet T-shirt contest, but she had refused to remove her bra and had been disqualified.

Braylon had come up to her after she'd been booted from the stage and commended her for not caving to the pressure of the crowd that had been yelling for her to "take it off." He'd then admitted that it would have made his night if she had listened to the crowd.

He'd left the bar with her phone number and a promise from her that she would actually pick up if he called. It was only after one of her girlfriends had remarked about the mark on his face that Leslie even registered it. She'd fallen in love with his eyes. They were so deep, by far the richest shade of brown she'd ever encountered. Both Cassidy and Kristi had been blessed with their father's eyes.

Leslie traced her finger down the cold glass in the frame, rubbing along Braylon's strong jaw. "We miss you," she whispered. "We miss you so much, honey. You would be so proud of the girls."

Her eyes fell shut and she tipped her head back. She tried to stop the hot tear that trekked down her cheek, but it had been an emotional day, and her defenses had plummeted to zilch. Besides, it had been a long time since she'd allowed herself to shed a couple of tears. She was due.

She looked down at the framed photo again.

"I'm sorry for some of the thoughts that have been

going through my head lately." Then she laughed. "You're probably more upset that I *haven't* had these thoughts sooner, but I warned you that I would have a hard time moving on."

The one thing Braylon had reiterated over and over was that if he didn't come home after one of his deployments he didn't want her to sit here languishing in sorrow. He wanted her to live on. He'd made her promise that she would find a good, loving father for his girls, someone who would protect them and vow to maim any boy who so much as dared to look at them with interest before the age of eighteen.

Leslie chuckled, shaking her head as she pushed back against the headboard and brought her knees to her chest.

Even though she had known it was a very real possibility that he could be taken from her, she had always felt deep in her heart that Braylon would return. She'd just never expected him to bring the kind of nightmares that followed him home from battle. Those scars—the ones etched on his soul—had led to his ultimate demise. He'd struggled with PTSD, had sought counseling both in the doctor's office and in the church, but it hadn't been enough.

Leslie's eyes fell shut.

These days it was only on the rare occasion that she allowed herself to think about Braylon's suicide. Wallowing in the tragedy wouldn't bring him back. It wouldn't give her girls a safe, stable home. The smart thing—the healthy thing—was to keep the good parts of his memory alive for both Cassidy and Kristi, and try her hardest to forget Braylon's tragic end.

But, God, it was hard to forget.

When it came to moving on, Leslie could only hope that one day she would find the strength to do it.

Unbidden, Gabriel's enticing smile strolled across her mind's eye.

How would she know when it was time to move on? How could she be sure? Was there something that would magically click in her head? Had it already clicked? Was that what those sensations she felt whenever she was near Gabriel was all about?

There was a danger to exploring this attraction that had sprung up between them, even if they'd vowed to be discreet. For the past two days she had tried to come up with an excuse to renege on her decision to get involved with him. But, as Gabriel had pointed out when Leslie had emailed him yesterday, there was nothing in any rule book that stated that a parent and a teacher could not date.

And, if she were honest with herself, she didn't want to back out. For the first time in longer than she could remember, Leslie felt electricity flowing through her veins. Just knowing that a handsome, sweet, thoughtful, sexy man was interested in her caused her skin to pebble with goose bumps.

"You're considering dating a child," she said, lowering her head to her knee.

Okay, technically, he wasn't a child; he was very much a man. But he was still Cassidy's teacher. What if word got out about them seeing each other? Would it be too weird for Cass? What if her classmates made fun of her? Cass had just started to come out of her shell after being terribly shy because of her birthmark. Leslie would never forgive herself if she somehow managed to set her back.

She could not do this to her little girl. As much as

it pained her, she would have to tell Gabriel that she'd made a mistake. She couldn't allow her own needs to come before Cass's well-being.

Stretching out on the bed, she ignored the nauseating feeling that settled in her stomach and tried to convince herself that she was satisfied with the decision she'd made.

Chapter 5

Leslie stared at the wooden gavel that, for the better part of her tenure as PTO president, had only been a showpiece. Tonight, she'd used it more than she had at all the other PTO meetings combined.

"Order, ladies and gentlemen, please," she called. "We must have some order if we're going to accomplish anything tonight."

For the most part the meeting had been civil, except for a contingent of parents who seemed hell-bent on ridiculing every single word that poured from Gabriel's mouth. Leslie didn't know if it had to do with his age, or if it was due to his being seen as an outsider, but she was shocked at the level of disrespect being lobbed his way.

Yet, despite the blows he'd taken, he'd held his own.

Leslie studied him as he responded to a rather nastily posed question about the new zero-tolerance bullying policy he'd implemented.

"What you call bullying, I call kids just being kids," Richard Lewis said. "How are kids supposed to build a thick skin if all they have to do is go running to the teacher every time they get picked on?"

"I agree with Richard," another parent said. "Mandatory suspension for a little harmless bullying is ridiculous."

"While I respect your right to hold that viewpoint, I don't agree with it," Gabriel said. "Take it from someone who has been height-challenged for much of his life—bullying is not harmless. Despite the fact that I was better on the basketball court than most of the kids in my school, I was still bullied because I wasn't six-two by the eighth grade. That stuff sticks with a kid much longer than any of you seem to realize.

"The students here deserve the safest learning environment that we can provide, and having to deal with a bully isn't safe. If it goes on long enough it can affect their ability to concentrate in the classroom, as well. I cannot sit back and do nothing if I know a student under my watch is being bullied."

There were grumbles from the audience, but Leslie also noticed quite a few parents nodding in agreement.

Leslie had never had sympathy for bullies, but this matter took center stage after she learned that Cassidy had been teased because of her birthmark. She'd vowed to be impartial, but when it came to this particular subject Leslie was unapologetically in favor of the zero-tolerance policy Gabriel had implemented.

The discussion finally turned to the issue that had necessitated the meeting in the first place: the school's annual Lock-In. Leslie sat in awed admiration as she watched Gabriel throw a preemptive strike that took the wind out of the majority of his detractors' sails.

"I understand there was a rumor that I wanted to cancel GEMS's beloved Lock-In. Let me start off by saying that this is one-hundred-percent false. I understand the importance of the Lock-In, both to the PTO's annual fund-raising goals and to student morale, but it's the student morale that I am looking to boost.

"The discussion that was overheard between myself and Principal Williams wasn't about cancelling the Lock-In. It was about adding learning-based games and activities and using them as a way to better prepare the students for the end-of-the-year state test. We can call it a Lock-In/Learn-In."

The murmurs got louder and had a much more positive tone.

"That's all well and good, Mr. Franklin, but honestly, the kids here work hard enough during normal school hours," Janice Taylor said. "The Lock-In is supposed to be fun."

The smile that pulled at the corner of his full lips did all kinds of wicked things to Leslie's pulse.

"Call me crazy, but I happen to believe that learning can also be fun," he said. "In fact, it *should* be fun. Take, for instance, the entrepreneurial booth Mrs. LeBorde is planning to set up. The students will be responsible for selling some of the snacks at the Lock-In/Learn-In. It's just one way that we'll be able teach a number of life skills like counting money, shouldering responsibility and being business owners."

The positive murmurs escalated along with some very enthusiastic head nodding.

Leslie had lived in this town long enough to recognize when something momentous was taking place before her very eyes, and to see how quickly Gabriel had won over this crowd was downright historic. As he continued his explanation of the various programs he'd proposed to Principal Williams, more and more parents fell in line. Janice even started a sign-up sheet, encouraging parents to volunteer for the Lock-In/Learn-In on the spot.

Leslie was in awe. Gabriel had this previously hostile crowd eating out of the palm of his hand.

And then, in five little words, everything went to hell.

"What about this merger business?"

Gabe stiffened with the shock of being caught completely off guard. He stood before the auditorium of parents whose faces were slowly starting to register alarm.

"What merger?" one of them asked.

"I heard that the school board wants to shut this school down and send all the kids to school in Maplesville."

The torrent of outrage that surged through the auditorium left Gabe breathless and filled with the sudden need to be anywhere but here. How in the hell had news of the merger gotten out? And who had said anything about closing the school?

Damn small towns and their rumor mills.

"How exactly are the students supposed to get to this new school?" one parent asked. "Are the bus drivers going to do double duty, bringing the elementary kids first, then following their same route to pick up the middle-school kids and drive them out to that new school?"

"I don't see why we need to break the elementary and middle schools apart. They've been combined for as long as I can remember," another parent said. "And what will this mean for the school mascot? Will they be the Maplesville Mustangs or the Gauthier Cubs?"

"Forget the mascot names—what about the name of the school itself? Is it going to have Gauthier in it or Maplesville?"

"Okay, okay," Gabe said, holding up both hands. "Can we calm down for just a second?"

He looked to Leslie, but she didn't appear in any mood to bang her gavel on his behalf. She looked as upset as the other parents.

Dammit! This was not how he wanted her to find out about the merger. It wasn't how he wanted *anyone* to find out. He and Principal Williams had discussed their strategic plan on how to introduce the idea to the community just yesterday. How was he supposed to gain the trust of parents if they thought he and the other administrators were keeping secrets?

"I know everyone has questions, but at this time I'm not at liberty to discuss anything regarding the potential merger," he said.

The crowd erupted again in a cacophony of angry outbursts, railing over the closure of the school. Many of the parents he'd had on his side just a few minutes ago were now shooting fire.

Gabe ran a hand down his face. He looked over at Leslie, afraid of what he would find staring back at him. But she wasn't looking at him; her focus was on the crowd and trying to calm them down.

"Order, please," she yelled while finally allowing her gavel to kiss the wooden table. "I know this is a change of events that no one anticipated, but if Mr. Franklin doesn't want to discuss it with us, we can't force him to."

"It's not that I don't *want* to discuss it," he quickly interjected. "I was asked to keep it under wraps until

Superintendent McCabe makes an official announcement."

His explanation didn't mollify the crowd one bit. Not that he was all that surprised. If he were in their shoes he wouldn't have been satisfied with that weakass excuse, either.

"We'll just have to take this to the school board," Leslie said. "They cannot close this school without a good reason, nor without first discussing it with the community."

"Wait," Gabe said. He could at least clear up this one major inaccuracy. "Let me make one thing clear. There are *no* plans to close the school," he said. "I can assure you, whoever said that got it wrong."

"It's not as if they haven't tried to close it before," Mrs. Taylor said. "We've heard the school board's sob story about the lack of money in the school system and how much would be saved if the children in Gauthier were bused to the schools in Maplesville. We've fought this fight and we are not fighting it again."

"Damn right!"

"Tell 'em, Janice!"

"Again, no one is talking about closing the school. GEMS will remain open," Gabe said.

"If they're not closing the school, exactly what are they doing?" another parent called out.

Gabe grimaced before he repeated, "I'm not at liberty to say."

The crowd reacted exactly the way he'd anticipated they would, exploding in another round of angry outbursts.

How had this turn into such a disaster so damn quickly?

He'd been in such a good place just a few minutes ago.

People had started to listen; some had even started to agree with him. Now it felt as if he was right back where he'd started, with the entire community against him.

He had to get control of this situation. If parents marched into the school-board office complaining about Mr. Franklin this and Mr. Franklin that, he could kiss that permanent assistant principal position goodbye.

Gabe could *not* allow that to happen. He'd already envisioned the look on Mr. Caldwell's face when he gave him the news during their monthly Skype chat. He'd already started searching for a nice, safe used car for Daniela for her high school graduation present, and he'd printed applications for three different private schools for Elias to attend in the fall.

He had to figure out a way to make this right. There was too much at stake.

"Give me a day to talk this over with Principal Williams and Superintendent McCabe," Gabe suggested. "I'll let them know that parents have questions."

"We have more than just questions," Mr. Lewis said. "We have opinions. A lot of them. And we don't need you to talk to the superintendent for us. We're the ones who put him in office. McCabe works for us. We can talk to him ourselves."

Leslie banged her gavel again. "Okay, folks," she began. "I know everyone is concerned about this merger or school closure or whatever it is, but storming into Mr. McCabe's office with pitchforks isn't the best way to get our voices heard. I think that we, as a board—" she held out her hands to encompass the people sitting with her at the head table "—should get together and evaluate everything that has been said tonight."

Gabe fought back a wave of apprehension as Leslie called the meeting to a close without acknowledging him. He couldn't really blame her for not having his back on this. He'd lied to her—a lie of omission was still a lie. He didn't expect her to join him in this quagmire he now found himself in.

At least her cool and calm demeanor had mollified the crowd. Gabe was grateful for that, at least.

The parents, including Leslie, filed out of the auditorium, talking among themselves and completely ignoring him.

Damn. Could this have turned out any worse?

Gabe made his way out to his car. He waved goodnight to a couple of parents still loitering in the parking lot, but only one returned the gesture. This was bad. This was more than bad; it was horrific. He wasn't back where he'd started in terms of gaining parents' trust; he was in a far worse position. Parents who had liked him—who had trusted him—were now against him.

As he opened his car door, a pearl-white compact SUV pulled up alongside him. The passenger-side window descended and Leslie called out to him from inside the car.

"Can we talk for a minute?" she asked.

Gabe braced his arm on the window ledge. "Are you sure you want to be seen talking to me? There are a few people still out here. They may think we're conspiring together."

"Gabriel, please get in the car," she said. "I've been dealing with the people here in Gauthier a lot longer than you have. I can handle whatever they dish out."

Gabe hesitated for the briefest second before opening the door and sliding onto the passenger seat.

Leslie's eyes remained forward, both hands wrapped around the steering wheel. She released a heavy breath before turning to him and saying, "First, I need you to be honest with me. What exactly is going on with this merger? Are they planning to close the school?"

"Absolutely not," Gabe said.

"Are you sure? Because there's been talk about closing the school before. The only reason it has never happen is because the parents here fought like crazy to stop it. You have to promise me that this merger isn't just a pretty way of saying a closure."

"I promise you, Leslie. GEMS isn't going anywhere. Well, the elementary school."

Her brow arched.

Gabe rubbed the bridge of his nose and released a weary sigh. The cat was out of the bag now; there was no need to keep this from her any longer.

He told her about the pilot program in conjunction with the department of education and how the new combined middle school would be a model for schools around the country.

"You still look skeptical," Gabe said.

"Honestly, it sounds fantastic," she replied. She shook her head. "But this school board has a track record. You have to understand something about life in Gauthier. We're a small town with an even smaller population, so we're often handed the short end of the stick. I've seen it happen time and time again. Gauthier gets passed over for towns that have more clout. But the one area we will never allow anyone to shortchange us is our schools. We only want what is best for our kids."

"Leslie, you have to know that I want the same thing. I have dedicated my life to educating children. My sole purpose here is to improve the lives of the students at GEMS. I promise you that I will never let anything get in the way of that."

Her expression softened as a gentle smile appeared on her lips.

"I believe you," she said. "I've seen you in action. I know that you have the students' well-being at heart."

Relief melted into his muscles. "Thank you for believing me, Leslie. I was so afraid that what happened tonight would ruin things between us before they even got started."

Her forehead creased in a frown. "About…us," she said.

"No," Gabe groaned.

"Gabriel, I have to consider how this would look if news of us being together got out."

"It won't. I told you, I can be discreet."

She pulled her full bottom lip between her teeth, worry haunting her beautiful face.

Gabe took her hand and brought it to his lips. "Leslie, please don't shy away from this. I'm willing to go along with whatever you want this to be—just let it be something."

The moments that passed as she stared at him were some of the most torturous of Gabe's life.

"Well, if you're up for it, why don't we get some *coffee* coffee?"

His face broke out into a smile. "It would be my pleasure, *cariño*."

Chapter 6

"So, let me get this straight. The Jazzy Bean, Lizzie's Consignment Shop and Pizza Mania didn't exist two years ago?"

"Nope." Leslie shook her head as she sprinkled sweetener through the steam billowing from her coffee mug, her lips tilting in amusement at Gabriel's shocked expression.

She perched an elbow on the tabletop, making sure to avoid the rough patches of worn laminate. A faint mixture of strong coffee and greasy fried chicken hung in the air of the tiny roadside diner where, for the better part of the past hour, Leslie had filled Gabriel in on a number of interesting facts about Gauthier.

"Half of the businesses on Main Street had closed down," she continued. "But then Corey and Mya Anderson discovered a room in the Gauthier Law Firm that was once used as a stop on the Underground Railroad, and everything changed. It put this little town on the map."

"That's amazing. Maybe Gauthier *will* get as big as Maplesville."

"I hope not," Leslie said. "I like having the convenience of the bigger stores in Maplesville, but I am just fine with Gauthier remaining small. I have to admit that my girls and I do love that new outlet mall out there, though. Probably too much."

"You're a city girl," he said with a laugh. "Of course you like the mall." His easy smile was devastating to her peace of mind.

"You're a city boy," she threw back at him. "Do *you* like the mall?"

"Absolutely," he said. "There is nothing I love more than mindlessly browsing store after store for hours on end every single Saturday. It kills me that I have to drive twenty whole minutes to get to the closest mall."

Leslie's shoulders shook with her laughter. "You've got jokes."

"I do all right."

Her own grin spread across her lips much more easily than it had during the past two years. She'd found herself laughing more tonight than she had in ages. Once she'd let her guard down, Leslie had discovered that she and Gabriel had much more in common than just their Houston roots.

At his suggestion, they had driven east to a diner in St. Pierre, a town that was tiny even by Gauthier standards. Other than a waitress with graying hair and a slight limp in her walk, and the cook behind the counter, she and Gabriel had been the only ones in here for the past hour. People in Gauthier rarely traveled this way, choosing to go either west toward Maplesville or south to Slidell. The chances of the two of them being seen were slim.

Because of that, she had been able to relax and just enjoy his company. And she *was* enjoying it. Immensely.

Leslie twirled the flat wooden stirrer through the foam covering her café au lait, making lazy swirls through the steamy south Louisiana staple.

"Besides having to drive *all* the way out to Maplesville to get your mall fix, how difficult has it been to adjust to life in Gauthier?" she asked.

He shrugged, picked up a shoestring French fry from the order they'd shared and dragged it through the ketchup on his half of the plate.

"Not difficult at all. As I said before, I was looking for a slower pace. Was it hard for you?" he asked, popping the fry into his mouth.

Her head tilted to the side, Leslie glanced up at him before drawing her attention back to her cup.

"It was at first," she admitted. "Probably because it was my first time leaving Houston. I went from being a girl who had never left home for more than a weekend trip, to being in a place that was so different from what I was used to that it seemed as if I was in a different country. It took some adjusting. It was even worse when Braylon would have to go back to base."

"He was Army?"

She nodded. "He served four tours in Iraq and Afghanistan."

"That must have been rough on you. I can't imagine going to bed every night wondering if I'm going to wake up to bad news." He paused for a moment, then in a gentle voice, asked, "When did the news come?"

When people who didn't know the circumstances surrounding Braylon's death inquired about it, they almost always assumed he'd been killed in action. At one time she would have just let them believe it, but over the past year she'd grown to accept that Braylon's death and the method in which he'd died were not her shame to bear. It wasn't her late husband's, either. He had been sick. There was no shame in that.

"Braylon wasn't killed while fighting abroad," Leslie said. "He suffered from PTSD. He committed suicide after he'd returned home."

Shock encompassed his face as he sat back in the green Naugahyde booth and let out a deep breath. Leslie held his gaze, refusing to give in to the urge to look away. His reaction to what she'd just told him would tell her a lot about the kind of person he was.

"Wow," Gabriel whispered. "I wasn't expecting that."

"Neither was I," Leslie said.

He reached for her hand, his eyes swimming with understanding and compassion instead of pity. It was just what she needed right now.

"It takes a strong person to endure that kind of pain and still come out standing," he said.

Strong?

It took everything Leslie had within her not to laugh at the notion of herself being strong. She wasn't strong, not even close. She'd put on a hell of an act for the people around here, though. She'd fooled everyone into thinking that she had bravely moved past Braylon's death. Even herself.

"I'm sorry if bringing up Braylon's suicide put a damper on tonight, but it feels better to have the truth out there."

He trailed the back of his fingers along her jawline, the soft caress featherlight. "Leslie, there is not a single thing you could say that would spoil tonight. When I say that this has been, by far, the most enjoyable night I've had since moving to Gauthier, know that it is the absolute truth."

His words stole the breath from her lungs.

"My goodness," Leslie said with an awe-filled whisper. "Do you have a book somewhere that teaches you the exact thing to say?"

He smiled that smile again, and her skin reacted in the way it had the first time she'd seen it. Tingles skirted along her nerve endings, eliciting all manner of decadent sensations to travel through her bloodstream.

The reasons she shouldn't be attracted to him were long and substantial, each item more significant than the next. He was six years her junior. He was her daughter's teacher. He'd made Gauthier his new home, and she was determined to leave.

But Leslie refused to acknowledge any of that tonight. For now, she would enjoy this feeling again, of being desired by someone she desired in return. It had been so long since she'd felt this way.

"You know what I noticed when we walked in here?" Gabriel asked. "There's pecan pie in that glass case on the counter. You think you can handle that?"

"Oh, yeah," she answered.

He went up to the counter and returned minutes later with a thick slice of pie and two forks. As they indulged in the flaky, buttery pastry, Leslie asked him about his time in New Orleans.

"How did you end up teaching in New Orleans?" she asked.

"The fraternity I belonged to at Texas Tech sponsored a cleanup event after Katrina. I spent spring break helping to rebuild a church in the Ninth Ward, then re-

YOUR PARTICIPATION IS REQUESTED!

Dear Reader,

Since you are a lover of our books – we would like to get to know you!

Inside you will find a short Reader's Survey. Sharing your answers with us will help our editorial staff understand who you are and what activities you enjoy.

To thank you for your participation, we would like to send you 2 books and 2 gifts – **ABSOLUTELY FREE!**

Enjoy your gifts with our appreciation,

Pam Powers

SEE INSIDE FOR READER'S SURVEY

For Your Reading Pleasure...

We'll send you 2 books and 2 gifts
ABSOLUTELY FREE
just for completing our Reader's Survey!

YOUR READER'S SURVEY
"THANK YOU" FREE GIFTS INCLUDE:
▶ 2 FREE books
▶ 2 lovely surprise gifts

PLEASE FILL IN THE CIRCLES COMPLETELY TO RESPOND

1) What type of fiction books do you enjoy reading? (Check all that apply)
- ○ Suspense/Thrillers
- ○ Action/Adventure
- ○ Modern-day Romances
- ○ Historical Romance
- ○ Humour
- ○ Paranormal Romance

2) What attracted you most to the last fiction book you purchased on impulse?
- ○ The Title
- ○ The Cover
- ○ The Author
- ○ The Story

3) What is usually the greatest influencer when you <u>plan</u> to buy a book?
- ○ Advertising
- ○ Referral
- ○ Book Review

4) How often do you access the internet?
- ○ Daily
- ○ Weekly
- ○ Monthly
- ○ Rarely or never

5) How many NEW paperback fiction novels have you purchased in the past 3 months?
- ○ 0 - 2
- ○ 3 - 6
- ○ 7 or more

YES! I have completed the Reader's Survey. Please send me the 2 FREE books and 2 FREE gifts (gifts are worth about $10) for which I qualify. I understand that I am under no obligation to purchase any books, as explained on the back of this card.

168/368 XDL GGFG

FIRST NAME   LAST NAME

ADDRESS

APT.#   CITY

STATE/PROV.   ZIP/POSTAL CODE

EMAIL

K-914-SUR-13

turned the summer of that same year and worked with Habitat for Humanity."

"That's amazing, Gabriel. I always said it was people like you who helped to put the city back together again after the hurricane. So many came from other places to pitch in."

"There was just so much need, I couldn't *not* help. My family wasn't swimming in dough—more often than not my mom would go without just so us kids could eat—but Katrina put things into perspective for me. Seeing so many people lose everything in the blink of an eye, it just made me that much more grateful for the little I did have. And it showed me that no matter how much I think I'm struggling, I can always do something to help someone less fortunate."

Leslie was so touched that she could barely speak past the emotion lodged in her throat.

"So much compassion in one so young," she said.

"I'm not that much younger than you," he said. "I thought we'd already established that."

The bell above the door of the diner chimed and Leslie's back stiffened. She quickly turned, her shoulders wilting in relief when she didn't recognize the couple that had just walked in.

Gabriel glanced at the door and then back at her. "You're really on edge, aren't you?"

"I can't help it," Leslie said. "Do you understand just how scandalous this is?"

"The assistant principal and president of the PTO? It would set the Gauthier grapevine on fire."

Leslie bit back a smile. "You're making fun of me."

"Just a little," he said.

"Have you always been this incorrigible?"

"That depends. Where does incorrigible rank on your list of traits you like in a person?"

"Nowhere."

"Well, then, I am not incorrigible at all, and I am offended that you would even suggest it."

A loud crack of laughter shot out of her mouth. She looked around, embarrassed, but no one was staring. No one cared that she was laughing out loud.

For the past two years Leslie had been so hyperaware of every display of outward emotion that she'd gotten to the point of showing none at all. She feared if she exhibited even a hint of sadness people would pity the poor Army widow. If she laughed too much they would think she was having too much fun for someone who'd lost her husband. Sometimes she felt like an emotionless robot.

But not tonight. Tonight, Gabriel had reintroduced her to the joys of letting go and enjoying herself. She'd missed this Leslie. It felt good to find her again.

"Maybe I haven't given that trait a fair chance," Leslie said. "Being incorrigible can't be all that bad, can it?"

He slowly shook his head. "It's not bad at all. I've found that being incorrigible gets me what I want."

She could feel his hot stare on her skin.

"And what is it that you want?" she asked.

Those lips turned up at the corners again, and her cheeks heated. She looked away, unable to handle the scrutiny of his hot, steady gaze.

"You're determined to get me in trouble, aren't you?" she said.

"Maybe you haven't given trouble a fair chance, either." He captured her chin and lifted it until her eyes met his. "In my experience, a little bit of trouble doesn't have to be a bad thing, *cariño*. In fact, it can be down-right good."

Leslie's heart drummed against the walls of her chest as Gabriel's mouth closed in on hers. A potent, intoxicating rush of sensation flooded her body at the first touch of his incredibly soft lips. Slowly, deftly, he laid siege to her mouth, applying just enough pressure to drive her wild.

A low moan climbed up from Leslie's throat and she gave in to the impulse to part her lips and let him inside. Once there, his tongue continued its gentle invasion, every swipe deliberate. Seeking. Devastating to whatever resistance she may have felt.

But resisting him was the last thing she wanted to do.

She curved her fingers around his neck, her thumb brushing faintly along his jaw as she encouraged him to move closer. Gabriel heeded her silent call, slanting his lips over hers and thrusting his tongue in and out of her mouth. Every lick, every taste was like manna from heaven, feeding her starved body with sensations she had not experienced in far too long. Leslie drank in his flavor, returning his decadent kiss with everything she had within her.

"Uh-hmm" came a groggy voice.

Leslie and Gabriel jerked away from each other. The waitress stood at their table, a coffeepot in one hand and their check in the other.

"Sorry to interrupt," she said. "But I wanted to make sure you paid the bill before you two cut out of here to look for the nearest motel room."

Leslie should have been mortified, but she was too satiated to feel even an ounce of embarrassment.

Gabriel handed the waitress a twenty-dollar bill and

declined the coffee refill. When his eyes returned to hers, they twinkled with devilment.

"You see? I told you trouble can be good."

Gabe tried his hardest to focus on grading the essay questions he'd posed to his fifth-grade class, but the high-pitched vocals of Jackie Wilson blaring next door stole every ounce of his concentration. He jumped up from the sofa and walked over to where his television was mounted. He banged his palm against the wall that divided the double-shotgun house he rented from Clifford Mayes, the sixtysomething-year-old who lived on the other side.

"I'm trying to work, Mr. Mayes. Can you turn it down?"

Several beats passed before Jackie's crooning about lonely teardrops began to dissipate.

Thank God.

Gabe had nothing against Jackie Wilson, per se, but he had an awkward relationship with sixties music. His dad had loved that era, and whenever Gabe heard music from that time period his mind automatically went back to those days of sitting next to the hospital bed that had been set up in their living room, he and his dad singing along with Sam Cooke, Solomon Burke and The Drifters. Singing eventually became too difficult for his dad, his deep baritone becoming nothing more than a weak, thready whisper during those final weeks.

Gabe ran a hand down his face. He had too much work on his plate today; any reminders of Gerald Franklin—even happy reminders—would put him in a headspace he didn't want to be in right now.

But Jackie Wilson's singing had unlocked the vault, and Gabe couldn't stop the deluge of memories from flooding his brain. He sank back onto the sofa and closed his eyes, making a valiant attempt to fight the memories but failing miserably at it.

Damn, but he missed that old man.

Gabe hadn't had a clue as to how taboo his mother and father's marriage had been: a twenty-one-year-old girl from Honduras marrying a black man from Houston nearly twice her age. He had never witnessed anything but love between them. His mother had been the happiest he had ever seen her during those days when his father had still been healthy. Gabe couldn't help but think about how different life would have been for him—for all of them—if cancer hadn't cut his dad's life short.

Of course, if his dad hadn't died, his mother never would have married Raynaldo, and his sister and brother never would have been born. He would not trade Daniela and Elias for anything in the world, but he would give his asshole of a stepfather up for a nickel. Hell, he would pay for someone to take him away from his family. Although, knowing Raynaldo, he likely wasn't around anyway.

Thinking about his loser stepdad, who could never stick around for more than a few days at a time, reminded Gabe that he hadn't talked to his mom all week. As he reached for his cell phone, it trilled with the ringtone he'd set for his mother.

"*Hola*, Mami," Gabe answered. "I was just about to call you."

His mother started in rapid Spanish, which was his first warning that something was horribly wrong. Other than calling her children the occasional endearment, his mother rarely spoke in her native tongue anymore.

"Wait, wait, wait," Gabe said, trying to get a word in. "What's wrong?"

"Your sister," she said. "She was supposed to be home three hours ago, and she is not answering her cell phone."

"Where was she going?"

"That's just it! She didn't say. She just left the house! I don't know what I'm going to do with that girl, Gabriel. She makes straight A's. How can I punish her?"

"It's her job to get good grades in school," Gabe said. "It's not her job to turn your hair gray. Let me try calling her, Mami," Gabe said. "She's probably out with one of her friends. I'll call you as soon as I hear from her."

"You tell her to call me."

"I will, Mami."

Gabe disconnected and immediately speed-dialed his sister's number. He massaged the bridge of his nose with his free hand, trying to stave off the worry that was building in his gut. His biggest fear with living six hours from Houston was that something would happen to his mother or one of his siblings, and he wouldn't be around to help.

Daniela answered on the second ring.

"Gabe. What's up?"

"Daniela, why did Mami just call me, frantic because she couldn't get in touch with you?"

He could practically see his sister's eyes roll as her tired sigh drifted over the phone. "I texted Elias and told him to tell her that I was fine."

"Why didn't you just answer when she called?"

"Because she would give me all kinds of shit if I talked to her."

"Watch your mouth," Gabe said.

"Oh, please. I'm seventeen."

Gabe lightly pounded his fist in the center of his forehead. He needed an aspirin. Or a drink.

"Call your mother, Daniela. She's worried sick about you."

"Ugh," his baby sister groaned. "That woman lives to spoil my fun."

That woman?

"You'd better show her some respect," Gabe said. "I mean it. If I get another call like that from Mami, I'm coming to Houston and carting you here to live with me in the sticks."

"I'll call her!" Daniela practically screamed.

"Where's Raynaldo?" Gabe asked. His mother shouldn't be the only one dealing with Daniela.

"Who knows? He dropped in on Sunday, but he was gone by Tuesday morning."

Gabe's jaw stiffened.

"I gotta go, Gabe," Daniela said. "I promise I'll call Mami."

Gabe tossed the phone on the old chest that served as his coffee table and leaned his head back on the rim of the sofa.

It was the same old story. It had been this way since his mother married Raynaldo Gutierrez the summer before Gabe started sixth grade, two years after his own dad died. Raynaldo had been worthless from the very beginning. He'd drift back home when he was out of money and needed a place to stay. All it took was a few halfhearted whispers of sweet nothings into his mother's ear, and she welcomed him back.

A couple of days later, the old tin coffee can where his mother kept her emergency grocery money would be empty and Raynaldo would be gone. By the time Elias was born, Gabe had been fourteen and done with his stepdad. The knuckleheaded crowd he'd fallen in with at school had convinced him that he didn't need some lowlife drifter telling him what to do. He was a man.

To prove it, on a dare, Gabe had broken into his science teacher's car one day after school. Instead of turning him in to the principal, or even worse, the cops, Mr. Caldwell had given Gabe a ride home. The next day, he'd asked him to stay after class.

The words Mr. Caldwell had spoken to him that day had changed Gabe's life. For the first time since his father, he'd had a male figure tell him that he was worth something. He had someone who believed in him. From that day forward, Gabe had been working to prove to his science teacher that he could be the man Mr. Caldwell had believed he was capable of becoming.

Aside from Gabe, Daniela and Elias didn't have someone like Mr. Caldwell in their lives. They actually had to rely on their own father to be a father to them, and Gabe knew that sure as hell wasn't going to happen anytime soon.

He cradled his head in his hands and tried to swallow back the guilt that was clawing at his throat. He needed to do more for them. His mother already worked two jobs; she could not do any more than she already was doing.

That was why he needed the assistant principal position to become a permanent thing. The boost in his salary would create stability for his entire family. It would lighten his mother's burden. It would alleviate the worry of wondering how to pay for the extra college expenses Daniela's scholarship didn't cover. And it would take Elias out of his current environment, a situation that was too much like the one Gabe had been in at that age.

"You have to find a way to make this work," he whispered.

It wasn't going to be easy, but he would do whatever he had to do to make that job his.

At least he knew he had one ally in his corner.

Just the thought of Leslie sent a flood of arousal coursing through his body.

He closed his eyes and relived every second of that kiss they'd shared at the diner the other night. The touch of her fingertips against the back of his neck, the rapid rise and fall of her chest as she'd took those breathy pants of air, the incredibly sweet flavor of her warm mouth as she'd opened it for him and sucked his tongue inside.

Gabe groaned and ran his hand against his aching groin.

He had anticipated what it would be like to kiss her for months, ever since the first day she'd walked into his classroom as a volunteer. Within moments of his mouth meeting hers, Gabe had decided that she had been worth every second of the wait.

He grabbed his cell phone and punched in her number.

"Hi," she answered. "What are you up to tonight?"

"Oh, nothing. Just grading papers and thinking about pecan pie. For some reason I can't get it off my mind."

"Neither can I," she said.

"Do you want me to make one and bring it over? I doubt it would be as good as the one we had the other night, but who knows? I might surprise myself."

She gave a nervous laugh. "Actually, I'm at The Jazzy Bean with a few parents from the PTO. We're putting together prize packs for the Lock-In/Learn-In."

"Oh, cool. I can come over and help."

The pregnant pause that filled the phone line was fraught with tension. "I think we have it under control," she said.

Understanding had Gabe's shoulders slumping in disappointment. Of course she didn't want him around when other parents were there.

Her insistence that they be discreet had not been that big of a deal. In fact, it had been kind of fun to slip away to that cozy little diner in St. Pierre, away from everyone they knew. But on nights such as tonight, when all he could think about was holding her close to him and tasting her lips again, their secret affair was the exact opposite of fun.

He wanted the freedom to be with her out in the open, where everyone could see that she had chosen him. There were no rules against them being together, nothing that said that he, as a teacher or school administrator, could not date a single parent.

But perception was everything, and if parents thought she was siding with him on issues concerning the school because they were seeing each other, it could make things awkward for her during her tenure as PTO president. She'd had enough to deal with the past couple of years. The last thing Gabe wanted to do was cause her discomfort.

So, instead of getting in his car and driving to the coffee house on Main Street, he returned to the papers he'd been grading and consigned himself to a night of wishing for what, at the moment, could not be.

Her feet curled underneath her, Leslie relaxed on the wooden swing that hung in the corner of her porch. This was *her* spot; it had been so since the day she and Braylon had moved into this house. How many evenings had she spent relaxing on this swing, the gentle sway lulling her into a state of calmness as she sipped lavender tea and decompressed from her hectic workday?

Today, it was both lavender tea and running her fingers through Buster's soft coat that provided the dose of contentment. There was no denying it; this little stinker was growing on her. The dog released a slight snore, and Leslie grinned. It looked as if the swing worked on canines, as well.

"Mommy?"

"Yes, baby?" Leslie asked, turning toward the front door at the sound of Kristi's voice.

"Can I please, please, *please* play Monster High on the computer?"

"You've put away those toys?" Leslie asked.

"Yes. And I put my socks in the drawer, too."

"Okay," Leslie said, planting a kiss on her forehead. She held up her watch. "You can play for thirty minutes. So what time will that be?"

Kristi studied the clock face. Telling time on a regular clock had proven to be more difficult for Kristi than it had been for Cass at this age.

"Seven o'clock," Kristi said, her face beaming.

"Good job."

"And then we can watch *Dancing with the Stars*," she said.

"You know it. Do you want Buster to come with you while you play?"

"No," Kristi said, shaking her head. "She just tries to eat the computer mouse. You can keep her." Kristi ruffled Buster's coat, then skipped back into the house.

"Send Cass out here," Leslie called after her. A couple of minutes later, Cassidy came out onto the porch.

"How's your science project coming along?" Leslie asked her.

Cassidy had begged her not to help with the science project, which was due tomorrow. She had insisted that she and Willow, her science-fair partner, could handle it on their own. The two of them had been on Skype all afternoon, even though Willow only lived two streets over. Kids.

"Are you sure you don't need any help?" Leslie asked.

"Yes, Mom. Willow and I know what we're doing. I promise."

"Okay," Leslie said, putting a hand up. "Just remember that I'm here if you need me."

"Can I go back into the house now?" Cassidy asked.

Leslie blew out a weary breath. "Yes, Cass."

Leslie tried to ignore the melancholy slowly creeping in, but it wasn't easy. Cassidy was exerting her independence more and more these days, and each time she did, it pierced Leslie's heart a little more. She missed her baby. And she knew it would only get worse as Kristi grew older, too.

Leslie heard whistling moments before she noticed someone out of the corner of her eye. She sat with her teacup arrested halfway to her mouth as she watched Gabriel leisurely walking along the sidewalk, hands in his pockets, a derby cap slung low over his brow. Her eyes tracked him as he strolled past her house, never once looking her way.

She set the teacup on the saucer and started to rise, but Buster protested with a yelp and she returned to her seat. The whistling returned, this time coming from the opposite direction. Once again, he walked right past her house, but just a few yards away, he stopped, pivoted and came back again toward her house. He turned and strolled up her walkway.

"So, did I convince you that I just happened to be walking in the neighborhood?" he asked.

"Is that what you were trying to do?"

"Kind of," he said.

Buster raised her head, let out a halfhearted bark, then put her head back on Leslie's lap.

"Quite the guard dog you have there," Gabe said.

"Don't let her extremely relaxed demeanor fool you. She'll attack your best pair of shoes and chew them to within an inch of their lives. So, why exactly were you trying to convince me that you just happened to be in the neighborhood?"

"Well, it wasn't you that I was trying to convince as much as any curious eyes that may be wandering and happen to catch us out here. Maybe they would think that I just so happened to run into you as I was taking a stroll in a neighborhood that's on the opposite side of town from my own.

"Is it okay for me to join you?"

She hesitated for the barest moment before she nodded. "Please do."

An easy smile spread across his lips as he climbed the steps and perched himself against the railing. Crossing his arms over his chest, he leaned back and looked from left to right along the tree-lined street. "It is a rather nice neighborhood," he said. "A lot nicer than where I'm renting."

He told her about the shotgun house where he lived not too far from the water-treatment plant.

"Mr. Mayes is a sweetheart," Leslie said. "At least you have a good neighbor and landlord."

"Except he's nearly deaf and plays his music loud enough for half the town to hear."

"A small price to pay for the chance to live next to one of Gauthier's former police officers."

"Seriously? I didn't know that."

She nodded. "For a long time he was the *only* police officer. After he retired the police station closed. Now it's only the parish sheriff's office."

Gabe shook his head. "I never imagined myself living in a town that's not big enough to sustain a one-man police force." He looked over at her and smiled. "It's a good thing it has other perks."

"Like?" she asked, her cheeks reddening.

"Oh, I can think of a few. Take the local PTO president, for instance. You don't find many of those who look—"

"Hey? That you, Leslie?"

She and Gabe both turned. Sawyer Robertson jogged in place on the sidewalk, his dark gray T-shirt stained with a V-shaped swath of sweat.

"Sawyer, hello," Leslie said.

He took her greeting as an invitation to come to the porch. Jogging up the steps, he ruffled Buster behind her ears and then stuck his hand out to Gabe.

"Hi there, I'm Sawyer."

"Gabriel." He looked between Leslie and Sawyer. "You live around here, Sawyer?"

"Just down the street," Sawyer said, nudging his chin west toward Willow Street. He turned to Leslie. "How did the hammock come out?"

"Oh, it's heavenly," Leslie said. "The girls and I love it. And we were able to hang it on our own."

"Well, if you run into anything that you can't do on

your own, just give me a holler." He nodded to Gabe before taking off down the porch steps.

Gabe ran his flat palms along his jean-covered thighs and let out a low whistle.

"So," he said. "Was that my competition?"

Leslie lifted a brow. "Are you trying to win something?"

"I thought that was obvious."

She smiled. "Consider yourself the victor. I have no designs on Sawyer Robertson."

"I think he has designs on you, though."

"He's trying not to disappoint a group of nosy church ladies who have been trying to find me a fine young man for well over a year," she said. "You don't have to worry about Sawyer."

Leslie studied Gabe's face for a moment and decided to share the realization she'd come to last night.

"You don't have to worry about anyone, Gabriel. Sawyer is one in a long line of gentlemen I've been introduced to in hopes that I would start dating again. But I've never felt even the slightest interest. Until you came along."

She saw his chest rise with the deep breath he pulled in. "Did you happen to borrow my book on saying just the right thing?"

"I didn't have to look at any book. It's the truth."

He rose from his perch on the railing and started for her, but stopped when the front door opened.

Cassidy walked out onto the porch.

"Cassidy! Hi," Gabriel said.

She looked from Leslie to Gabriel, her forehead furrowing in confusion. Then her eyes grew wide with horror.

"Did I fail my quiz today?" she asked.

"No, sweetheart," Leslie said with a laugh. "Mr. Franklin just came over to discuss something about the PTO."

Her daughter was too smart for her own good, given the way she still looked from Leslie to Gabe with that hint of skepticism in her eyes.

"If you say so," she said, her voice dripping with the same incredulousness that was clouding her face. "I was just coming to tell you that *Dancing with the Stars* is starting."

"Thanks, baby. I'll be in in a minute. Why don't you pop the popcorn?"

Cassidy nodded and then gave Gabe the once-over again before returning to the house.

"Dancing with the Stars?" he asked, eyes alight with amusement.

Leslie shrugged. "What can I say? We're a household of reality TV junkies. The girls especially love the dance shows. *Dancing with the Stars, America's Got Talent, So You Think You Can Dance?* They've become weekly events."

"I'm jealous. Mr. Mayes never wants to watch *Dancing with the Stars.*"

She stared at him and then burst out laughing.

"If you keep up with all that laughing, you're bound to draw attention to us," he said. He moved from the railing and slid in next to her on the porch swing, lifting Buster from her lap and placing the sleeping dog in his own. "What would the neighbors think if they saw us having so much fun?"

"Well, unless they passed directly in front of the house, they would have a hard time seeing anything. Between the fig tree on one side and the shadow cast by the sun on the other, we're pretty hidden."

"Hmm, you make a good point," he said. "So maybe we don't have to worry about nosy neighbors getting the wrong idea."

"Is there a wrong idea?" she asked. "Maybe they would think that Cassidy's teacher is so diligent that he makes house calls. Or that the assistant principal and president of the PTO are talking school business. Since, you know, that's what we're doing."

He inched closer. "What if I don't want to talk school business anymore?" he murmured. "What if I want to do something that has nothing to do with school?"

"And what would that be?"

His eyes smoldering with want, he leaned in and captured her mouth in a kiss that was surprisingly, achingly sweet. Leslie yielded to his mouth with amazing ease, dropping every guard and opening herself to the pleasure he wrought within. A slow burn of desire crawled its way from her feet up through her entire body the moment Gabriel's tongue swept over her lips.

God, she'd missed this. Even though it had only been a few days since the last time he'd kissed her, she'd missed it terribly. She missed the intimacy, the closeness, the feeling of being wanted and desired. And she could feel in every insistent thrust of his tongue how much he wanted her.

Leslie opened her mouth wider, accepting all there was to his kiss.

She felt Gabriel's fingers inching up her arm, coming to rest on her shoulder before moving to her face. He cradled her cheek in his hand, his touch so light, yet so heavy with meaning.

Yearning for more of him, she thrust her tongue into his mouth, moving it back and forth along his tongue, soaking in every bit of his flavor. Her hand skirted up his chest, and she was shocked at the response in her own body. Tingles skidded all over her, rushing to the spot between her thighs. It pulsed with need, dampened with desire as his skillful mouth laid claim to her.

Arousal quickened within her, driving the need to feel him against her. She skimmed her hands underneath the hem of his shirt, relishing the warmth of his skin, the light dusting of hair across his stomach. Every nerve ending within her body prickled, sang with an electricity that had her on the verge of begging him for more.

But, God, she couldn't have more. Not here with her daughters on the other side of that door.

Just as she was about to pull away, Gabriel beat her to it. He released her lips and hopped up from the swing, still cradling Buster in his arms. A ragged breath rushed out of him.

"Okay, I had to stop myself while I was still able."

Leslie nodded her understanding. She pressed the back of her hand to her lips, which throbbed with sensation from the feel of his incredible mouth.

The front door flew open.

"Mom!" Kristi called. "You're missing the first dance!"

"I'll be there in a minute, honey," Leslie called, but her eyes remained on Gabriel.

What was he doing to her? How, after all this time, was she suddenly *feeling* again? He made her feel *so* much. Happy. Excited. Alive.

Scared.

Lord, but he scared her. Because for the first time in far too long, she could feel her heart slowly opening again. Her heart still ached from the last time she'd allowed that to happen.

He set Buster in her lap and pressed a chaste kiss to her forehead.

"You're thinking way too much," he whispered, his warm breath making her skin flutter. "Stop thinking so much and just let this happen, Leslie. I'll see you later."

And with that he was gone, leaving her with the memory of his sweet kiss to get her through the night.

Chapter 7

"Mr. Franklin, you're needed in the library," Ardina's disembodied voice sounded through the PA system.

Wincing, Gabe gathered the signs he'd just printed and carried them with him to the library. The minute he walked in he spotted Mrs. Roussell, the school librarian, who had graciously allowed them to hold part of this year's science fair in her sacred domain, waving him over to the circulation desk.

"You needed something?" Gabe asked.

She pointed toward the alcove that had the giant tree sprouting books for leaves painted on the wall. It was where the kindergartner's story time was usually held.

"There aren't enough tables for the Earth and Space Science category," she said.

"But we set up eight tables."

"You've got twelve solar systems, Mr. Franklin.

They take up twice as much space as the regular science projects."

Gabe cursed under his breath. Who knew organizing one little science fair would be such a headache?

"I'll try to round up a few more tables. In the meantime, see if we can't squeeze them a bit closer." He held up the papers. "I just have to get these signs laminated and on the tables, and I'll be back in here to help finish the setup."

He exited the library and nearly ran smack into Leslie.

"Whoa there," she said, catching him by the wrist. "Take it easy, Mr. Franklin."

"Sorry," Gabe said. He took a step back and instantly regretted the distance he'd put between them. "How is your morning going?" he asked. "Have I thanked you already for being here?"

"My morning is going fabulously, and of course I'm here," she said. "The PTO always provides doughnuts and coffee for the Science and Social Studies Fair judges."

"Thank you for that, too," he said. "Now I understand why that Lock-In is so important. The PTO foots the bill for just about everything around here."

"We *are* a stellar PTO. We're the kind of PTO other PTOs envy," she said.

"I'll bet," he said, laughing at the sass in her voice. "GEMS is lucky to have you all."

"Oh, no, you're the one GEMS is lucky to have," she said. "At least that's what your colleagues think." She hooked a thumb over her shoulder. "I heard a few of them talking back there while I was setting up the refreshments in the teachers' lounge. They're impressed. They said the science fair has never been so well organized. I do believe you're making a positive impact on this place, Mr. Franklin."

Gabe knew it would be impossible to put into words what it meant to hear her say that. Knowing that he was making a difference was everything to him. *Everything.* Some mornings, it was the only thing that got him out of bed, recognizing that there was a school full of impressionable kids who needed a role model they could look up to, like he'd had with his own science teacher.

He was in the position to be a Mr. Caldwell for the two hundred and fifty children at Gauthier Elementary and Middle School. He'd been given the opportunity to be a positive influence in so many lives.

And he was doing it. He was succeeding. God, that felt good.

"Mr. Franklin," the voice sounded over the PA system again. "You're needed in the music room."

Gabe pointed down the hallway. "That's where the physical and applied science projects are," he said.

"Yes, that's where Cass and Willow are presenting their project. I've been warned not to come within ten feet of the room."

Gabe took a couple of steps, bringing them closer. "In case you were wondering, I don't feel the same way." He lowered his voice. "You can come as close to me as you want to today."

The classroom door across from them opened and the language-arts teacher, Jean Gardener, came into the hallway. Leslie jumped away from him as if he was on fire, and a nasty feeling instantly pooled in Gabe's stomach.

"Hi, Leslie. Mr. Franklin," the teacher said as she walked past them.

"Hi, Mrs. Gardener," Leslie returned. She waited

until Mrs. Gardener was out of earshot before she turned back to him and said, "I'm sorry about that."

Gabe lifted a shoulder, the epitome of nonchalance. "Forget about it," he said. "We have a deal, don't we?"

"Gabriel," she said, her shoulders sagging with remorse. The regret he heard in her voice mollified his disappointment to a certain degree, but it didn't stop the nausea from churning in his gut. He didn't like feeling as if he was something she was ashamed of. But he didn't like seeing the sorrow in her eyes, either.

"Really, Leslie. It's okay," he said, the need to put her at ease greater than his own hurt and anger. "You just have to let me know when I *can* see you again."

Pulling her bottom lip between her teeth, she looked up and down the hallway. "I'll have a few free hours once this school day ends," she said. "Shayla is taking the girls shopping as a reward for Cass getting through the science fair."

"I'll take it," Gabe said.

He wanted to kiss her so damn bad he ached with it, but he knew she wouldn't allow it. Hell, *he* wouldn't allow it. Dating the parent of one of his students was one thing. Kissing her in the hallway was another.

"Good luck with the fair," she said.

"You, too," Gabe replied. He caught her by the hand before she could walk away. "You know that old abandoned gas station on the west side of Maplesville?" he asked. She nodded. "Meet me there at three-thirty. I promise it will be worth the drive."

Several hours later, Gabe and Leslie pulled up to the Abita Mystery House in Abita Springs. The town was known for its brewery, but its off-the-wall museum had been on Gabe's list of places to visit for months.

"What are we doing here?" Leslie asked.

"Have you been here before?"

"No."

"Yeah, well, I figure a lot of the people in Gauthier never think of visiting this little gem." He got out of the car and ran to the other side to open her door. "Not a huge chance of us being seen."

"Ah, okay," Leslie said as she alighted from the passenger side. "I could have probably come up with a dozen other places."

"But do any of those places have a silver Airstream trailer that was visited by aliens?" Gabe asked.

He shut the door with his hip and grabbed her by the hand, leading her to the entrance of the museum, which was an old filling station circa the 1950s, complete with the gas pumps. The place looked more like a junkyard than a museum, but at least it had character.

They strolled through exhibits of eclectic folk art, dioramas of New Orleans city streets and even a house whose exterior was completely made up of thousands of shards of glass. The cleverly titled House of Shards was the first exhibit to elicit a positive reaction from Leslie. At least Gabe thought that was a smile he saw on her face.

"It's obvious this isn't your cup of tea," Gabe said as they visited Darrell, the half dog, half alligator creature that guarded a collection of random pieces of barbed-wire fence. Gabe had to admit Darrell was a little too strange even for him.

"I think we've found something we do not have in common," Leslie said. "I am not into old and weird."

"Let me just visit the Airstream, and we can leave," he said.

She flung out her arm. "Lead the way."

"Here it is," Gabe said, rubbing his hands together as they came upon the silver, bullet-shaped trailer.

"This is what you came all the way to Abita Springs to see?"

"Yes!" He knew he had the goofiest smile on his face, but he couldn't help it. "Do you know the story behind the Airstream and the aliens?"

"To be honest, I had no idea this place existed until we pulled up to it," Leslie said. "I'd never even heard of it."

"Seriously? You're not a fan of sci-fi, are you?"

"I'll let you in on a little secret." She leaned in close. "I've never seen a single episode of *Star Trek*."

Gabe flattened his palm to his chest. "You're killing me here."

Her eyes glittered with amusement. "Try not to hold it against me."

"I promise I won't," he said, returning her smile. "It's just that I don't know what I would have done without those stories back in high school. They probably saved my life."

She tilted her head. "*Star Trek* saved your life?"

"Not just *Star Trek*. David Brin's Uplift books, Octavia Butler's Patternmaster series. Once I discovered them, I devoured them. They kept me off the streets. Who knows what kind of trouble I would have found myself in if I hadn't been introduced to books?"

He saw the hesitation in her eyes before she asked in a soft voice, "Did you get into a lot of trouble in high school?"

He huffed out a cynical snort. "Me and trouble? We were best friends," he said. Gabe shrugged a shoulder as if it was no big deal, when, in fact, outside of Tristan, no one else in Gauthier—in all of Louisiana—knew about his past. "I didn't get along with my stepdad. Fell in with the wrong crowd. Turned into your typical little punk."

"What changed?" Leslie prompted.

"I got caught trying to break into my tenth-grade science teacher's car." Gabe shook his head. "For some reason he thought I was worth saving instead of being sent into the system. He's the one who introduced me to science and books and everything else that's made me into the man I am today."

Tender understanding shone in her brown eyes. "He sounds very special."

"He is," Gabe said. "We still keep in touch. I talk to him at least once a month. I just wish my baby brother had someone like that in his life." He looked up at her. "I'm afraid for him, Leslie. I'm afraid he'll get caught up in that life. That's why I need this assistant principal position to be permanent. I need to help my family. The extra money that promotion would bring would help me send Elias to another school—a better school."

"One with a thousand sci-fi books at his disposal?"

He caught the amusement in her voice. "Yeah, something like that. Although, I'm not sure I could ever get Elias to read a sci-fi book. He's more into biographies and boring nonfiction." He shook his shoulders in an exaggerated shudder. "Not sure where the kid gets that from."

"There's nothing wrong with that," Leslie said with a laugh. "I don't read sci-fi, but I'm a big reader, too. Mysteries mostly. I love trying to figure out the whodunit before the big reveal."

"So we're both lovers of the written word," Gabe said, coming to stand in front of her. He wrapped his arm around her waist and pulled her in close. "It looks as if we discover something else we have in common every day. And to think you were willing to let something as trivial as our ages come between us."

"Silly me," Leslie said.

He used her words from earlier. "I won't hold it against you," he said, his lips a hairbreadth from hers. He lowered his mouth and, just before kissing her, whispered, "You've more than made up for it."

Leslie twisted the length of twine around the cloth napkin and set it in the middle of the gold-trimmed bone-china plate. She moved the wine goblet a few inches to the left, then went around the table and did the same to the other five place settings.

"When is Xavier's family getting in?" she called to Shayla, who was in the kitchen putting the finishing touches on the Italian cream cake she'd baked for dessert.

"Their flight gets in around four, but by the time they get through baggage claim, pick up the rental car and drive in from the airport, they probably won't get here until after six o'clock."

"Are they staying at Belle Maison or was Xavier able to convince them to stay here with you all?"

"Nope, they're still staying at the bed-and-breakfast. Xavier's grandfather said he doesn't want to impede the process just in case the two of us come to our senses and decide to have a baby," Shayla said with a laugh. She came in to the dining room and her face instantly beamed. "This looks amazing, Leslie. I swear, you need to start your own decorating business or something."

"Anyone who knows how to look things up on Pinterest can do the exact same thing," Leslie pointed out.

"Do I need to remind you of my last attempt at re-creating something I found on Pinterest?"

"That's okay. Kristi told me about the sock puppets you two tried to make. She said the puppet needed to go to the dentist."

"She's right. That poor puppet had the ugliest smile I've ever seen. Sewing buttons in a half-moon isn't as easy as it looks."

Leslie laughed as she set a mini wildflowers bouquet at each place setting.

"Okay," Shayla said, "What exactly is up with you lately? There's something different about you. You seem…I don't know…happy."

Leslie's brows spiked. "Do I normally look un-happy?"

"That's not what I'm saying. You're just more… bubbly lately."

"I'll make a note to be more bubbly from now on."

Shayla rolled her eyes. "Would you stop it? I'm just making an observation."

Leslie hesitated for a moment, before she said, "Okay, if I tell you, you have to promise not to go all crazy on me."

Shayla's eyes widened. "What did you do?"

Leslie pulled her bottom lip between her teeth, then said, "I sort of went on a date. Actually, several dates."

Shayla squealed.

"Shh," Leslie admonished, pointed to the living room, where the girls were.

Shayla clamped her hands over her mouth, then lifted them and whispered, "Who? Was it Sawyer Robertson? Please tell me it was Sawyer! The minute I found out that he moved back to Gauthier, I knew he would be perfect for you. You're the same age. You're both pro-fessionals—"

"It isn't Sawyer Robertson," Leslie said.

Shayla's forehead furrowed. "Are you sure it's not Sawyer?"

Leslie released a nervous laugh. "I'm pretty sure I remember who I'm dating."

"Well, if it isn't Sawyer, who is it?" Shayla asked, as if Sawyer Robertson was the only man in all of Gauthier that Leslie could be interested in.

Leslie hesitated for a moment before admitting, "Ga-briel Franklin."

Shayla's eyes grew so wide Leslie was sure she would need to manually pull down her eyelids. "As in Cass's teacher, Gabriel Franklin? The one with the great ass?"

Leslie nodded.

"You go, girl!" her sister-in-law said, excitedly clap-ping her hands. "Good choice."

"Be honest, Shayla. You know this is not a good idea," Leslie said.

"Why not?"

"As you already pointed out, he's my daughter's teacher, but that's just the tip of the iceberg. Let's not even talk about the fact that he's a child."

"He is not. He may be a little younger than you, but he's not *that* young." She shrugged. "I wouldn't have pegged him as your type, but if it works, why not?"

"What's my type?" Leslie asked, unable to keep the hint of defensiveness out of her voice.

"Well, you *were* married to my brother, who was one of the most serious people I've ever known. Mr. Frank-lin seems so much more laid-back."

"He is different from Braylon, but that's not necessarily a bad thing, is it?" Leslie fell into a seat at the table and covered her face in her hands. "God, Shayla, what am I doing?"

"You're moving on," her sister-in-law said. Leslie didn't resist when she felt Shayla's hands prying her fingers away from her face. "There is absolutely nothing wrong with moving on, Les, and if the young, hot Mr. Franklin is whom you chose to move on with, more power to you, girlfriend. You could do a lot worse. That tight butt alone should make it all worth it."

"What are you doing looking at his butt?"

"Every female eye in Gauthier has snagged a glimpse at that butt." Shayla kissed her pinched fingers. "Perfection."

Leslie's head flew back with her laugh.

Growing up with two older brothers, Leslie had never known what it was like to have a sister. She'd been close to her female cousins, but it wasn't the same. Braylon's death had forced Shayla and Leslie to confront their issues. It had not been easy, but the two of them had finally found a place where they were both comfortable in their relationship. Now Leslie couldn't imagine life without her.

A familiar pall slid over her. She would have to adjust to life without Shayla if she returned to Houston.

The pounding of little feet on the hardwood floor drew both Leslie's and Shayla's attention.

"We've got the flowers," Cassidy said, holding a vase filled with Late Purple Asters they'd picked from Shayla's backyard garden. Kristi held up a bunch of yellow weeds.

"I liked these instead of the purple ones, but Cass wouldn't let me put them in the glass jar," she said with a pout.

Leslie took the weeds from her hands. "I have the perfect place for them," she said, taking the mason jars she'd put on the table to hold the dessert forks and putting the flowers in them. "There. Perfect."

With her hands on her hips, Kristi turned to her older sister and gave her a haughty nod. Then, with her nose in the air, marched back to the living room. Cassidy just rolled her eyes.

The minute they were gone, both Leslie and Shayla burst out laughing. They worked together putting the finishing touches on the table. Then Leslie went into the living room to collect the girls.

"I want to stay for the party," Kristi said, clamping her arms over her chest and showcasing another stellar pout.

"It's a party for grown-ups," Cassidy said. "It's gonna be boring."

"Hey," Shayla said with mock affront. "Grown-ups know how to have a good time."

Cassidy gave her an unconvinced look.

Leslie pulled Kristi to her side. "How about we have our own party tonight?" she asked. "We can bake cookies and watch a movie. But first, you girls have to bathe Buster."

"Can I take a bath with Buster?" Kristi asked.

"No," Leslie answered. "Buster has to take her own bath."

"And don't get me wet this time," Cassidy warned.

"Sounds like fun times in the Kirkland house tonight," Shayla said with a laugh. "I'm almost sorry I'll miss it."

"You won't miss anything. Those two will end up getting in a fight, and I'll end up giving Buster a bath. It's our typical Saturday night."

With another laugh Shayla enveloped her in a hug. "Thanks again for helping. Of course, I'm going to tell everyone that I did it all by myself." She cupped Leslie's shoulders in her palms and gave them a firm squeeze. "Remember what I said. You deserve this—whatever this is you have going with Mr. Cute Butt."

Leslie sent her a grateful smile. "Thank you, honey. Good luck with the in-laws tonight."

Shayla waved that off. "Compared to my other in-law, this set is easy."

Leslie stuck her tongue out at her as she ushered the girls out the door.

The rest of the night turned out just as Leslie had predicted. Moments into Buster's bath, Kristi accidently—or so she claimed—sprayed Cassidy with the sprayer, which instigated a fight between the girls. Instead of baking cookies and watching a movie, they were both sent to their rooms after dinner, and Leslie was stuck grooming Buster.

As she dried the dog with a fluffy bath towel, Buster turned to her and licked her nose.

"I still don't want to like you," Leslie said. "I don't care how cute you are—you're not going to win me over."

Buster scarfed at her, wringing a laugh she had been determined not to give the little runt.

"I guess you're not all that bad," she said. "You're actually starting to grow on me." She rubbed the towel behind the dog's ears. "I wasn't sure I could adjust to having you here, but it turns out I'm starting to adjust to a lot of things I never thought I would be able to handle."

Releasing a sigh, Leslie set Buster on the floor and, bracing her hands on her thighs, pushed herself up. On legs that trembled slightly under the weight of what she was about to do, she walked over to the closet in her bedroom and opened the doors wide.

She stared at the clothes hanging on the right side of the closet. For two years the suits, dressed shirts and starched blue jeans had hung neatly next to hers. But their wearer would not be returning.

Swallowing past the ache in her throat, Leslie pulled hangers out one at a time, removing the clothes and laying them flat on the bed. She was halfway through the closet when she came upon Braylon's dress uniform.

She dropped her face into her hands, her shoulders shaking as she silently wept. Quiet sobs racked her body, stealing the breath from her lungs as she remembered all the times she'd watched him get into that uniform. Handsome. Brave. Proud.

How lucky she'd been to have him in her life.

But he was gone, and because of Gabriel, she could finally see a new future in front of her.

Leslie moved the uniform to her side of the closet. It was the one thing she could never part with, the one piece of Braylon she would allow herself to hold on to.

As for everything else, maybe if she finally let go of it all, she could finally move on.

Chapter 8

Gabe grabbed an apple from the bowl the school counselor kept on her desk, taking a loud bite as he made his way out of the front offices. He headed for the teachers' lounge, hoping the turkey sandwich he'd stored in the fridge two days ago was still good. Eating his lunch after classes had already ended for the day wasn't ideal, but his normal lunch period had been usurped by an emergency meeting with the parent of a student who had been caught cheating and had been given after-school detention.

Gabe could remember back to when he'd gotten in trouble in school. His mother always listened to both sides, but tended to give the adult the benefit of the doubt. Those days were a thing of the past. Now the parents he encountered thought their kids could do no wrong. Every teacher and administrator was out to get them.

It didn't help that he was still at the very top of most parents' hit list.

Shaking his head in frustration, Gabe backed his way into the teachers' lounge, which was busier now that students had been released for the day. Some were gearing up for the extracurricular activities they sponsored, while others were preparing their work for tomorrow.

As he made his way to the refrigerator, Gabe sensed several sets of eyes on him. He also noted that there had been a definite drop in the volume of conversations. He glanced at the table where two of the kindergarten teachers sat, along with Chantal Wayne, who taught second grade. He smiled and waved. The gesture wasn't returned.

Dammit.

What had he done to piss people off now?

From the moment he'd been placed in the interim assistant principal position he'd anticipated teachers being somewhat jealous. It was only natural. Here he was, an outsider who hadn't even been at the school a full year, coming in and suddenly being in a position of authority. To Gabe's surprise and relief, his colleagues had taken the transition with ease. They'd respected his new position and hadn't treated him any differently than they had before he'd stepped into his new role.

But there was nothing warm and fuzzy about the vibes he was picking up right now.

Gabe left his turkey on wheat on the top shelf in the refrigerator and turned to the table of teachers.

"Hey, Chantal, do you have a few minutes to discuss the Lock-In/Learn-In event?" he asked.

She glanced at the two kindergarten teachers, hesitated for a moment, then said, "Not right now. I'll email you."

That pretty much confirmed that something was off.

Chantal had taken the lead on the Lock-In/Learn-In. She was always eager to discuss it.

Gabe needed to talk to his person on the inside so he could figure out just what the heck was going on here. He took off for Tristan's class, catching him just as he was packing up his sheet music.

"Hey, man," Gabe said. "You got a minute?"

"For you? I don't know," Tristan said. "Not sure I want to be seen speaking with the enemy."

Gabe dropped his chin to his chest. "I knew it," he said. "I wasn't just imagining those cold shoulders I got in the teachers' lounge a minute ago."

"When people who trusted you find out you've been holding out on them, it sometimes rubs them the wrong way."

Gabe held up his hands, stupefied.

"One of the teachers at Maplesville High let the cat out of the bag," Tristan said. "The school is buzzing about proposed cuts to the staff due to the merger. And word is that you knew all about it. I can't believe you've been holding out on me, man. I thought we were boys."

"I have no idea what you're talking about. I haven't heard anything about cuts to the faculty."

Tristan shrugged. "It's not as if it was unexpected. You can't have a merger and not get rid of some staff."

"Why not? It's the same number of students. Some will just be in a different facility."

His friend shrugged again. "It fits the narrative the school board has been trying to write here for a while. I wouldn't be surprised if word comes down that they're closing GEMS. That's what they really want to do."

Gabe vehemently shook his head. "No, no, no," he said. "I don't understand why people keep saying that. No one is closing the school."

If this school closed, not only would he not get a permanent assistant principal position, his head likely would be on the chopping block when it came to faculty cuts. Of the teachers here, he was the newest. The last one to walk in the door was always the first one out.

"It's hard not to jump to the worst-case scenario," Tristan said as he zipped up the flat case he used to carry his sheet music. "The school board has a track record when it comes to Gauthier."

Leslie had said the same thing, but Gabe didn't care what the school board had tried to do in the past. Closing GEMS was not on the table. He couldn't help it if the people in Gauthier were paranoid. He only knew what he had been promised by Superintendent McCabe, and he couldn't very well be the new permanent assistant principal of a closed school.

As for teachers losing their jobs, Tristan was right, it was probably inevitable. The assumption that those cuts would come from GEMS didn't sit well with Gabe at all. Leslie had told him that the people here were used to getting the short end of the stick; it was only natural that they would believe that the same would happen this time around.

Not if I have anything to do with it.

He made his way back to his office, his footsteps slowing as he approached the teachers' lounge. But he didn't have the authority to discuss anything with the teachers. Hell, he didn't know enough *to* discuss anything with them. Neither McCabe nor Principal Williams had said anything about teachers' jobs being cut.

He needed to talk to the superintendent as soon as possible so he could set teachers' minds at ease. He'd discovered just how quickly rumors could fly in this small town, and if word got out that GEMS would lose teachers in this deal, Gabe would find himself in a stickier situation than he was in already.

And that was something he could *not* permit. He barely had anyone in his corner as it was; he sure as hell couldn't lose any more support.

It was like déjà vu.

Hadn't it been just a couple of weeks ago that he'd stood before a group of angry parents railing at him because of a rumor that had gotten completely out of control? When he'd called Leslie and asked to get on the agenda for the monthly PTO meeting to address the current rumor regarding GEMS teachers losing their jobs, he'd hoped that it had not spread too far yet, seeing as he'd just heard it from Tristan a few hours ago. But small towns and all that.

Leslie had barely called the meeting to order before Reshonda Cochran, the mother of students in both his fourth- and fifth-grade science classes, stood and, ignoring the agenda's order of business, brought up the subject of the school merger and potential job losses.

"Not only did I hear that it would be only teachers from GEMS that would be cut, but I also heard that Principal Williams is being replaced, too."

The murmurs in the crowd grew louder and more agitated.

Gabe put up his hands. "Wait, wait, wait. I can't speak on any changes to the faculty regarding teachers, because I simply don't know, but I can assure you that Principal Williams's job is safe. In fact, Principal Williams will be over the newly merged middle school."

This reveal set off a round of excited murmurs around the room.

He knew he wasn't supposed to say anything, but

neither Williams nor McCabe was here fielding questions from this hostile crowd. If he could find a way to set their minds at ease regarding this merger, he was going to use it.

"What about the mascot? Will it be the one from our school or the one from Maplesville?" another parent asked. Gabe was pretty sure it was the same parent who had asked about the mascot at the last meeting.

"I still don't know. Maybe they'll hold a contest to come up with a brand-new mascot." Now that he thought about it, that wasn't such a bad idea. He'd bet the students would really get into something like that.

"I want to know about the PTO," Janice Taylor asked.

"What about the PTO?" Leslie asked.

"This PTO currently serves both elementary and middle-school students. Some of us have kids in both age groups. Once the middle schools merge, will we have two separate PTOs? Will we have to join in with the PTO at Maplesville Middle School? What's going to happen?"

Leslie's forehead dipped in a frown. Apparently, she hadn't thought that far. Gabe hadn't, either. It was a legitimate question that would have to be answered, but he could only handle one crisis at a time.

"I guess we'll cross that bridge when we come to it," Leslie said. "We're all adults and we all have the children's best interest at heart, whether they are from Gauthier or Maplesville. I'm sure we'll figure something out."

The voice of reason saved the day yet again.

She had the perfect temperament for this position. Gabe was pretty sure he'd have given up by now if anyone else on this PTO board were president.

He managed to get through the rest of the meeting

unscathed. Someone brought up the anti-bullying initiative, but he'd apparently convinced enough parents during the last meeting that it was a good thing. Several in the crowd spoke up in favor of it.

After the meeting finally ended, Gabe was approached by one parent after another. He tried his best to assuage the fears and concerns many still had.

He looked around for Leslie, his chest tightening in concern at the realization that she'd left the school without speaking to him. Had he missed something? She hadn't seemed upset at him, which had Gabe even more confused.

As he walked to his car, his phone chirped with an incoming text. His shoulders sank in relief after reading it.

He got into his car and drove around the main building. He pulled alongside the huge green garbage containers between the cafeteria and field house, then cut the engine. A few minutes later he spotted headlights in his review mirror.

Leslie's white SUV pulled up alongside him.

Gabe unlocked the passenger-side door and waited for her to get in.

"Just give me one minute to text the girls' babysitter," she said. Her fingers flew across the touch screen. When she was done she tossed the phone into his cup holder, leaned over and caught him by surprise with a deep, smoldering kiss.

"Wow," Gabe said once she'd sat back on her side of the vehicle. "Thank you."

"I've been wanting to do that all night."

Gabe chuckled. "I wasn't talking about the kiss, although I thank you for that, too. I meant for having my back in there. You could have sided with the audience."

"I didn't really side with anyone," Leslie said. "But I need you to be honest with me, Gabriel. What do you know about the faculty cuts?"

"I swear to you that I don't know anything. I only learned about this rumor earlier today when I walked into the teachers' lounge and found myself the recipient of the stink-eye. And, let me tell you, they give a mean stink-eye here in Gauthier."

Her lips twisted in a subtle smirk. "I know," she said. "I've gotten it a time or two myself, usually when I walk into church late."

"Late-for-church stink-eye is the worst stink-eye."

Her smile widened. "Let's hope this is the last of it that you'll see. I know the people here seem overly concerned about this, but you can't really blame them."

"If they were not concerned about what is happening to their kids, that's when I would start to worry. I think we put some minds at ease tonight, though."

"I think we did, too," she said.

He leaned over and nuzzled her neck, nipping the spot behind her ear. "We seem to make a pretty good team."

"You think so?" she asked. Then she gasped.

"Oh, yeah," Gabe said. He gently tugged her toward him and closed his mouth over hers.

The kiss went from sweet to scorching before he could catch his next breath. The moment Leslie's desperate moan escaped her throat, Gabe was gripped with a hunger so fierce it consumed his every thought. He plied her with his tongue, thrusting it deep into her hot, wet mouth.

His hand sought her breasts, coasting from one soft, supple mound to the other. He felt her nipples grow stiff under his touch and he got hard. Instantly hard. *Painfully* hard.

Gabe's mouth moved from her lips to her throat, while his hands went lower. He skimmed his fingers along her thigh and then cupped her bare knee. Her legs parted ever so slightly, giving Gabe all the invitation he needed to continue on his quest. He ran his palm up her inner thigh, the skin so deliciously warm and smooth he had to stop himself from diving headfirst for a bite. He traced a path up her thigh to the spot between her legs, finding it as hot and damp as he'd imagine.

A groan tore from her throat as he moved her soaking panties to the side and slid his finger up the wet folds. Or maybe *he* was the one who groaned. The sounds resonating around the car became so loud and desperate Gabe couldn't tell who made what.

With unrelenting fervor, he stroked in and out of Leslie's pulsing center, slipping two fingers deep inside her while the pad of his thumb massaged the tender nub of nerves at her cleft. As his fingers penetrated her, his tongue continued its exploration of the delicate skin at her throat. He licked and sucked and nipped, soaking in every bit of her flavor.

He felt her body tighten around him and knew she was close to the brink. Gabe pulled out one wet finger and circled the knot again before he pinched down on it, imagining the throbbing nub inside his mouth instead of between his fingers.

Leslie's back bowed off the seat and she screamed at the ceiling. Her chest rose and fell as she sucked in one deep breath after another.

Gabe caught hell trying to get control over his own breathing. He hadn't been so close to coming while still completely dressed since he was fifteen years old.

"Oh, my," Leslie breathed. "I can't believe I just did that with my daughter's teacher. And behind the school cafeteria, for goodness' sake."

"It's okay," Gabe said. "I'm the assistant principal. I can get you out of detention."

She looked over at him and burst out laughing. Her beautiful face was still flushed from the massive orgasm that had torn through her. Damn, how he wished he could give her another one this very second. All it would take was a little maneuvering. He could push the seat back, slip onto the front-passenger floor and lose himself in that warm, wet heaven between her legs.

"Go out with me," he said.

Her brow dipped in a cautious frown. "What?"

"Go out with me," Gabe repeated. "On a real date. Not some rendezvous at that dive in St. Pierre or behind the school cafeteria. I want to take you out on a *real* date, where we get dressed up, go out and have a good time like a normal couple."

"Gabriel—"

"It doesn't have to be in Gauthier. As a matter of fact, there's nothing in Gauthier that will fit what I have in mind." The caution in her eyes turned to curiosity. "Just say yes, Leslie. I'm asking for one real date. That's all."

After a beat she nodded. "Okay. What about this Saturday?"

"Really?" he asked, hope blossoming in his chest.

"Yes," she said. "Shayla is coming to pick up the girls Saturday morning after we get back from the Lock-In/Learn-In. They're spending the night at her house."

A smile drew across Gabe's face. "Saturday night it is. I'll pick you up at seven."

Chapter 9

Leslie sent Stewart a message reminding him that she was leaving early, then packed her briefcase with the documents she would have to work on over the weekend. Just as she was about to shut down her laptop, Stewart responded with a request for her to step into his office on her way out.

Leslie rapped lightly on the opened door and peeked in. "You wanted to see me?"

"Yes, yes. Come in," Stewart said. He tossed the pen he was holding onto the desk and gestured for her to take a seat.

Leslie had yet to bring up the potential transfer to The Woodlands office. She could do so right now if she wasn't such a coward.

"I have a proposition for you," Stewart said before she could speak. "As you know, we've had a couple of really good quarters and when I was at headquarters a couple of weeks ago, I discussed a possible expansion. The guys in New York agreed."

"Agreed to what?"

"A second location. Our North Shore clientele has been steadily growing, so much so that it warrants a satellite office. There is retail space available in a new development in Maplesville that would be ideal, and I think you would be the ideal person to run it."

Leslie's back went ramrod straight.

"What's with that look?" Stewart asked. "You don't agree?"

"Well, yes, I guess I do. It's just that I wasn't expecting this."

"This is perfect for you, Leslie. You would be required to check in with this office at least one day a week, but much of your time would be spent running the satellite office in Maplesville. You would be closer to your daughters and it would cut your commute in half, wouldn't it?"

"At least," Leslie said.

She was absolutely stunned by this turn of events. She'd come into Stew's office debating whether or not to bring up a transfer. She didn't think *he* would be the one talking about a transfer—and to Maplesville, of all places. On a good day she could be at the office in fifteen minutes flat.

"I have every confidence you can handle this, but I also recognize that it entails more responsibility than you may be up for right now. Don't give me an answer just yet. Take the weekend to think it over."

"I only get the weekend? When exactly would this move happen?"

"That retail space has been going at lightning speed. I convinced the rental manager to hold the space for me for a few days, but if we're going to do this, then we have to act on it. Like I said, take the weekend."

Leslie nodded. "I'll let you know Monday."

She walked to her car on autopilot, her brain swirling with everything she'd just learned. She slid into the driver's seat and just sat there for a moment gripping the steering wheel.

What in the heck had just happened?

For months now she had been mentally preparing herself to leave this office—but for Houston, not Maplesville. Her reasons to pack up her family and move had been slowly dwindling over the past few weeks. Now Leslie was hard-pressed to remember just why she had felt such an all-consuming need to leave Gauthier at all.

But she was smart enough to recognize that her reasons were being outshined by her new relationship with Gabriel, and this amazing opportunity Stewart had just dropped in her lap. Just because she could bring herself to finally pack up Braylon's clothes and donate them to the Goodwill didn't mean that she was ready to face the next fifty years living in that house, living in that town.

She had her reasons for wanting to leave. Eventually, they would rear their ugly heads again, and this nice glow would all but dissipate.

A couple of hours later, Leslie found herself standing in the complete chaos that was GEMS's annual Lock-In, now known as the Lock-In/Learn-In. More than two hundred and fifty kindergarten through seventh-grade students filled the gymnasium, their noisy chatter and laughter reaching decibels that could rival that of a jet engine taking off.

Parents and teachers worked in shifts to chaperone. The first were here from 7:00 p.m. to midnight. The second shift would come in at midnight and stay until 7:00 a.m. Last year Leslie had foolishly taken the second shift, thinking it would be the easier of the two.

Wrong.

As the night had dragged on, many of the smaller children eventually had fallen asleep, but the older kids had stayed awake and wired throughout the night.

As this year's PTO president, Leslie didn't sign up for a specific shift. Even though it didn't officially fall under her responsibilities, she still felt it her duty to make sure everything ran smoothly throughout the event. So she would be in and out during the night, hopefully catching a few catnaps on the sofa in the teachers' lounge. She wanted this year's Lock-In/Learn-In to be the best yet.

She acknowledged that a huge portion of her need to make this year's event a success was due to Gabriel being so invested in it. She believed in his quest to have the lock-in do double duty, giving the students a chance to have fun and learn at the same time.

As she ambled around the gymnasium, Leslie had a feeling they were well on their way to reaching the outcome Gabriel had envisioned. The gym was sectioned off according to class subject. There was a fierce competition between two teams of sixth graders to see who could solve a prime-factorization puzzle the quickest.

In the reading corner, blankets, sleeping bags and pillows had been set up, creating the perfect space for cuddling up with a good story. It warmed Leslie's heart to see so many kids taking advantage of the books that had been donated by The Book Nook, a new independent bookstore that had just opened in Maplesville. Meanwhile, the kindergartners—including Kristi—were undeniably enthralled with whatever story Mrs. Guidry was reading to them. Leslie waved, but her daughter's rapt attention was focused solely on the young teacher.

Leslie didn't need but one guess to figure out where she would find Cassidy. If Kristi was enthralled with Mrs. Guidry, Cassidy was completely enraptured with Mr. Franklin.

Leslie looked toward the spot that had been cordoned off for the science fun and games. Gabriel stood at the head of a table surrounded by a bunch of excited students. He held beakers of clear liquid in each hand. In dramatic fashion, he raised the beaker in his right hand and began pouring the liquid into the other. The two clear liquids met to create a yellow cloud.

The students' reaction was priceless. They clapped and cheered as if it was the most amazing thing they had ever witnessed in their lives. For some, it probably was.

Gabriel looked up and caught her staring. A subtle, skin-tingling sexy smile edged up the corner of his mouth. Leslie tried to look away, but it would have been easier to convince every one of these children to go to sleep at this very minute than to convince her eyes to look anywhere but at this gorgeous man who made her body hum with electricity each and every time he looked at her.

She continued to observe him as he returned to the table filled with various science paraphernalia: beakers, Bunsen burners and his prized microscope. He glanced over at her and waved for her to join him. She pointed at her chest and mouthed, *Me?*

Gabe shook his head and pointed past her. Leslie turned and spotted her brother-in-law striding across the gymnasium floor.

"How's it going?" Xavier asked, giving her a kiss on the cheek.

"What are you doing here?" Leslie asked, returning the kiss.

"Mr. Franklin asked me to come in and do a presentation on some basic physiology." He held up the large black case in his right hand. "I've got my intestinal-system dummy. It's always a hit at parties."

Chuckling, Leslie patted his back. "I hope you and your dummy have tons of fun."

She forced herself to focus on other aspects of the Lock-In/Learn-In so that she wouldn't be tempted to sneak peeks of Gabriel. He was always sexiest when he was in pure science-geek mode.

She joined the volunteers working the concession stand and found herself in the middle of a heated debate on how much cheese was appropriate to pour on the nachos. She was preparing to duck flying hot *queso* when she caught Elora Boudreaux motioning for her to come over. The older woman, who had at least a dozen grandchildren attending GEMS, was in charge of doling out prizes for the various games.

"Please tell me there are more prizes for the kindergarten through second-grade kids," Mrs. Boudreaux said, wringing her hands as if a lack of prizes would be the end of the world. Although, for this bunch it just might be.

"There should be," Leslie said. "Let me check the storage room. We stored them away from the gymnasium because we didn't want to have too many of them out at one time."

"I can get someone else to get them if you're too busy," Mrs. Boudreaux said.

"Oh, no!" Leslie said. She lowered her voice and leaned toward the other woman. "I don't want to go back to the concession stand."

Mrs. Boudreaux put a hand up to shield her mouth, then whispered, "I understand. I've run concession with Belinda at the basketball games. That woman is power hungry, and she'll take it wherever she can get it."

Leslie checked around to make sure none of the other age groups needed prizes before leaving the gymnasium. Just as she reached for the door to the main building, she heard someone call her name.

Leslie turned and found Gabriel jogging up the covered walkway that connected the gym to the rest of the school.

"You skipping out on the Lock-In?" he asked. "Too much noise for you?"

"You think I can't handle that?" She hooked a thumb toward the gym. "I have a five-year-old, a nine-year-old and a dog. That's nothing."

"It makes me appreciate Mr. Mayes and his music," Gabriel said. "It sounds like a beehive in there."

"Don't worry. By the end of the night you'll be so used to it that you won't even hear it."

He nudged his chin at the door. "Where were you going?"

"I'm on prize-restock duty. We'll have a kindergarten mutiny on our hands if I don't bring out more lighted yo-yos and Frisbees."

"Do you mind company?" Gabriel asked.

Leslie's eyes narrowed with suspicion.

He put both hands up. "I swear I just want to help."

"Fine. You can help," she said. "Just remember that there's a gymnasium full of students just steps away, so no funny business."

"I promise," he said, a wickedly seductive smile tipping up the corners of his lips. He opened the door and motioned for her to walk ahead of him. The moment they entered the school's storage room, Gabriel caught her wrist and spun her around, pinning her to the door.

"I didn't realize you were so gullible," he whispered against her lips.

Leslie returned his smile. "It looks as if it worked to my advantage."

He caught her other arm and entwined their fingers. Amusement glittered in his eyes as he closed the distance between them, bringing his chest flush against her breasts. He lowered his head and took her lips in a kiss that had every fiber of her body humming with need.

If not for the door holding her up, Leslie would have melted into a puddle right on the floor. She pressed her body into his as he pushed his tongue into her mouth, swirling it around, sucking on her bottom lip. His hands moved from her wrists to her shoulders, then down her back. Gabriel cupped her backside, fitting her soft center against his swelling hardness.

The moan that climbed from her throat was drenched with want.

How much longer would she be able to hold out? Why did she even want to? Her body was screaming for her to give in to this need that had begun to consume her nearly every waking moment since the first time he'd kissed her. She would be foolish not to take advantage of everything he could do to her.

And, goodness, did she want him to do things to her. She wanted him to do things to her until she couldn't walk straight.

He moved his mouth from her lips and trailed it along her neck. Leslie's head fell back against the door. She ran her hands up and down his back, pulling him even closer, the need to connect her body with his instinctual. Primal.

But they couldn't give in to those primitive desires. Not here.

"Gabriel, we need to stop," she murmured against his lips, but it was the exact opposite of what she wanted. She didn't want this to stop. She wanted it to go on and on until they were both naked and exploring every square inch of each other.

But there was a gymnasium full of people, including her two daughters, just steps away.

Leslie brought her hands around to his chest and gently pushed. He raised his head. His expressive eyes were dazed, their brown depths flooded with a passion that made her want to say to hell with where they were and just tear off his clothes. But she knew better.

"We can't do this here," Leslie said. "Anyone can walk in."

He nodded and took a step back. "You're right," he said. He let out a shaky laugh and brought his hand up to rub the back of his head. "That wasn't supposed to go that far. I swear it was only supposed to be a quick kiss."

"We haven't mastered the quick kiss," she said. "Every kiss we have seems to last longer and longer."

That smile she was starting to crave crept up the side of his mouth. "I don't know about you, but I don't have the desire to change that anytime soon. I'm growing rather fond of our very long kisses."

"So am I," she said, her cheeks heating to unprecedented levels. "Just not when half the town is a few yards away." She brought her hand up to her neck. "There are no marks, are there?"

He peered at her neck. "Umm…" He pulled his bottom lip between his teeth.

"Oh, God." Leslie slapped her hands over either side of her neck. "Please don't tell me I have a hickey."

"You don't." He laughed, holding his hands up. "I was kidding."

"Gabriel," she said in a warning tone.

"I promise there is no hickey," he said, leaning over and placing a light kiss on her cheek. He whispered in her ear, "Your secret love affair is safe."

The slight tension she heard in his voice gave her pause. Even though he hadn't said anything, she knew he was growing increasingly uncomfortable about keeping their relationship a secret. She studied his face, but his expression betrayed nothing.

"How many prizes do you want to bring over?" he asked, motioning to the bins of toys.

She regarded him for another moment before answering, "Fifty or so should be enough." Leslie reached for the plastic bin, but he blocked her with a hand.

"I've got this," he said.

She stood idle as he went about loading the prizes into canvas shopping bags. She wasn't sure what to make of what had passed between them after their kiss. Should she bring up the discretion thing? Was she ready to hear what he had to say about it?

Despite whether his feelings had changed regarding the secrecy of their relationship, hers had not. Leslie wasn't ready to face the questions from her girls or the whispers from the people in Gauthier, whom she had no doubt would have an opinion about her dating a man so much younger than she was. Especially when the single, handsome, more age-appropriate Sawyer Robertson was right there, waiting in the wings.

No, she was not ready to face that battle.

From the beginning, Gabriel had said he was willing to take whatever she was willing to give. Leslie could only hope that those words still held true, because if his feelings had changed then she would have to give him up.

And the thought of doing that hurt more than she'd ever thought possible.

As he pulled into Leslie's driveway, Gabe couldn't help the smile that broke out over his face. For the entire drive he had vacillated between feelings of relief, accomplishment, pleasure and validation. He had so many emotions flooding his bloodstream, he didn't know *what* to feel.

Pleasure. He would definitely go with pleasure.

Because when he'd called and asked Leslie where she wanted to meet him for their date, she asked that he pick her up at her house. She wanted him to come to her door like a regular boyfriend. Like someone she wasn't ashamed to let the neighbors see on her arm.

Yes. Pleasure. He was feeling much, *much* pleasure at the thought of Leslie finally being comfortable with the idea of being seen out in the open with him.

Gabe lifted the dress he'd bought for her from the backseat and started for the house.

Damn if he didn't want to skip up her walkway. He was just that excited about tonight. This woman couldn't possibly know how hard he'd fallen for her.

When Leslie answered the door, Gabe had to take a moment to just soak her in.

"God, you look amazing," he said, his eyes roaming over the sleeveless pale pink sundress and strappy sandals. He tilted his head to the side and frowned as he followed her inside. "Unfortunately, you'll need to lose everything but the jewelry," he said.

Her brows shot skyward. "Excuse me?"

Gabe held up the garment bag. "I figured you wouldn't

have the appropriate outfit for where we're going tonight, so I took the liberty of buying it for you."

"You bought me a dress?"

He nodded, then gestured to her outfit. "While what you're wearing is gorgeous on you, you're going to need something a bit more flamboyant when you learn the salsa tonight."

"You're taking me dancing?"

The way her eyes lit up made Gabe instantly regret that he had not thought to take her dancing before tonight. To have her look at him like that, he would take her dancing every night.

"I want to see what *Dancing with the Stars* has taught you."

She grabbed the bag from him, her eyes glittering with excitement.

"Give me five minutes," she said before dashing out of the room.

While she changed, Gabe roamed around her living room. There were several doggy chew toys strewn about the dark brown hardwood floor. The oval coffee table held several magazines, three remotes and a picture of stick figures that Gabe assumed was Kristi's handiwork. She'd drawn Leslie, Cassidy and herself, along with the dog. Gabe's smile sobered when he noticed the other stick figure among the clouds. Her father.

He walked over to the large framed photograph above the fireplace. Leslie was seated on a stool, holding a baby who could not have been more than a year old. Cassidy, with her hair in curls and two front teeth missing, stood just to her right. A serious-faced man, dressed in a uniform that was covered with patches over the left breast, stood behind them, one hand on Leslie's shoulder and the other on Cassidy's.

Gabe stared at his face. The dark birthmark Leslie had mentioned was prominent, but for some strange reason it seemed to suit Braylon Kirkland.

Gabe was torn between feeling sorry for him and, in the same breath, grateful that he wasn't here. If the man in that photograph were still alive, Gabe wouldn't be taking Leslie salsa dancing tonight. Yet, again, he knew how much Leslie had suffered after her husband's death. How, in many ways, she was still suffering.

Selfishly, Gabe decided he was okay with the way things were.

He knew she loved her husband and missed him terribly, but she was a young, vibrant, sensual woman. Nothing was going to bring Braylon Kirkland back. She needed to move on with her life, and he wanted to be the one she moved on with.

He heard Leslie's footsteps and quickly stepped away from the portrait. He didn't want her to know that he'd even noticed it. Discussing her dead husband was not on his agenda tonight.

However, when she walked into the room, Gabe didn't have to pretend that he hadn't seen the photo. One look at Leslie and he couldn't remember a single thing he'd seen this past week.

She walked up to him and turned, showcasing her slender back.

"Do you mind zipping me up the rest of the way?" she asked.

"Yes, I do," he said. "I'd rather help you *out* of this dress, not into it."

She turned and gave him a chastising frown, but the playful twitch at the corner of her mouth betrayed her.

"Turn around," Gabe said. He groaned when he realized there was no bra strap across her back.

She looked back. "What's wrong now?"

"No bra," he choked out.

The blush that swept across her cheeks was so sexy, so damn adorable, it made it even harder to resist peeling the dress off her body and exploring every supple inch. Gabe's hand shook with need as he gently glided the zipper up her back, his soul weeping with every inch of that smooth skin that was covered by the fabric.

Once he was done she held her hands out and twirled, her eyes focused on the ruffled hem that flared around her thighs. Gabe was more taken by her gorgeous legs and how soft they looked. He wanted to feel those legs around him so badly he was ready to drop to his knees and beg her to forget leaving this house.

But the excitement in her eyes stopped him. She deserved the fun that awaited her tonight.

"This dress is perfect," Leslie said. "How did you know what size to get? Was it just an extremely lucky guess?"

"Well, not really," Gabe said. "I have this same dress in two other sizes in my trunk. I'll bring them back to the mall on Monday."

Her eyes widened before she burst out laughing.

"I can't believe you went through all this trouble, but I'm happy you did." She put a hand on his shoulder and kissed his cheek. "Thank you. I love it."

Gabe captured her chin and turned her to face him. He gently tugged her forward and covered her mouth in a slow, tender kiss. As his eyes fell shut, he tried like hell to forget about the bed that was just a few yards away, and all the things they could be doing in it right now.

She was worth the wait. He had to remember that she was worth the wait.

Less than an hour later Gabe parallel parked into a spot on Frenchmen Street, only steps away from the club he'd discovered in the Faubourg Marigny neighborhood of New Orleans back when he'd first come to the city to help in the cleanup following Hurricane Katrina. Because it was one of the highest points in the city, the neighborhood, which was adjacent to the French Quarter, was one of the first areas to recover from the devastating hurricane.

Gabe would take the Marigny over the French Quarter any day of the week. Unlike the Quarter, which was filled with tourists doing their best to re-create the wild image they had of New Orleans from watching too many *Girls Gone Wild* videos, Farbourg Marigny had a relaxed, laid-back vibe. If he had not taken the job in Gauthier, this was likely the neighborhood he would have moved to.

He rounded the front of the car and opened the door for Leslie.

The sight of her legs in those shiny black heels sent an arrow of lust straight to his groin. He immediately added dragging his tongue down her legs while she wore nothing but these black pumps to his bucket list. His life would not be complete unless he experienced that.

How in the hell was he supposed to get through the next four hours of dinner and dancing? It would be agony.

But it would be worth it.

"I hope you don't mind having a light dinner," Gabe told her. "But if you're going to learn to salsa, you don't want a five-course meal weighing you down."

"I'm afraid to eat anything at all," she said with a

laugh. "I'm too nervous that I'll make a fool of myself once the lessons start."

He pressed a swift kiss to her lips. "Even if you did you would be the most delectable fool to ever grace a dance floor. But it doesn't matter because you're not going to make a fool of yourself. You've been studying, remember? Watching all those episodes of *Dancing with the Stars* was homework."

"Oh, sure. Lying on the couch watching other people dance has totally prepared me. You're going to pretend you don't know who I am when we start dancing."

"That would never happen. Do you know how long I've been waiting to tell people about this sexy, amazing woman I've been dating?"

Her eyes softened. She trailed her fingers along his chin.

"You've been so understanding. I hope you know just how much I appreciate you respecting my wishes, Gabriel."

He cupped her bare shoulders and tugged her closer.

"I won't lie, Leslie. It's been more difficult than I first thought. But it's easier than the alternative. Do I want to shout it from the rooftops that I'm falling in love with you? Hell yeah, I do. But I won't say anything until you're ready. I can wait."

"Did you just say you're falling in love with me?" she asked.

Gabe's breath caught in his throat. Damn, had he said that too soon?

"Does that freak you out?" he asked.

She held his gaze, her eyes searching his. After several long moments she slowly shook her head.

"No," she said on an awe-filled whisper. "It doesn't."

Relief. Pleasure. Validation. They were all there

again, fighting for position within his heart. Once again, pleasure won out.

Gabe tilted up her chin and kissed her forehead. "It's time for me to show you the night of your life. Prepare to dance until you drop."

They ducked into The Three Muses, just one of the dozens of eclectic bars and restaurants that lined Frenchmen Street. They were lucky enough to find two seats available at the far end of the bar, the perfect spot to enjoy a quick bite.

When Leslie ordered a beer from the tap, Gabe fell the rest of the way in love with her. Just like that, he was done. She was the woman for him. No need to look anywhere else.

Leslie had only eaten half of the yucca fries and tempura shrimp she'd ordered for dinner when she pushed it away and said, "Okay, enough of this, I'm ready to dance."

"The dance lessons don't start for another twenty minutes." Her frustrated pout wrung a laugh out of him. "How long has it been since you've gone dancing?" Gabe asked.

"Goodness, I can't even remember. It was definitely before Cass was born."

"You haven't been out dancing in nine years?"

"Never had the time," she said with a shrug. "We didn't have much help in the way of babysitters. Shayla was in Seattle and my family was in Houston. Once Braylon's deployments started, it became even more difficult. When he was home on leave we never took the time to go out, just the two of us. He offered, but I knew how much he missed the girls and how much they missed him. It seemed selfish to ask for a night just for myself. I thought there would be enough time for that when the girls were older and he was out of the Army."

"He was a soldier," Gabe quietly pointed out. He didn't want to sound insensitive, but he had to say it. "You had to have known that there was a chance his time would run out. War is dangerous."

"Yes, but only one of Braylon's tours was on the front lines. He was in logistics, so he stayed within The Green Zone most of the time, setting up communications and such. He was as safe in Afghanistan as he was anywhere else. But it still took a toll. He saw so many soldiers leave and not come back, and so many come back missing limbs. It was just too much for him to handle."

"It was a lot for you to handle, too, wasn't it?"

The sadness that shone in her eyes caused his lungs to tighten with pain.

"It was." Her chest expanded with the deep breath she took, then she smiled, overly bright, and said, "But I got through it. There's something to be said for making it out of that time in my life without collapsing under the weight of all that pressure."

Gabe just stared at her for several moments, awed by her strength. "You are so incredible, Leslie. The more I learn about what you went through, the more I'm amazed by the woman you are." Gabe took her hands in his and pressed a gentle kiss to her fingers. "I feel so lucky to have found you."

"I feel the same way about you." She cupped his jaw and leaned in for a deep, soul-stirring kiss that left him craving her taste. "You came into my life just when I needed you," she said. "We're lucky to have found each other, Gabriel."

He was so in love with her. He would never understand why it took him so long to realize it, even though, in reality, they had only been together a few weeks. That didn't matter. His body was weak with the love he felt for her.

"Gabriel," she whispered.

"Yes?"

He felt her smile blossom against his lips. "I'm ready to dance."

Gabe's smile traced hers. "Let's give the lady what she wants."

He cashed out with the bartender and, taking her by the hand, guided her next door to The Blue Nile. There was already a crowd forming in the long-standing nightspot that was popular with locals who appreciated the laid-back atmosphere.

"I've never been here before," Leslie said. "Although, I can say that about every bar that lines Frenchmen Street."

"Are you serious?"

She lifted her shoulders in a hapless shrug. "It's sad when I think about it, but in all the years I've lived in Gauthier I can count on one hand the number of times I've come into New Orleans for something other than work. I've just never taken the time to do it."

"How can you live so close to New Orleans and not take advantage of all the things there are to love about this city? You know what this means, right?" She shook her head. "We're going to take this drive every weekend for the next year if necessary. You are going to experience New Orleans the way she is meant to be experienced."

An odd look flashed across her face, and Gabe immediately wanted to take back his bold statement. He'd already admitted to her that he was falling in love with her. He didn't want to freak her out by making plans for their next year together.

Baby steps. They would have to take baby steps.

Thankfully, they were saved from the awkwardness that had suddenly sprung up between them by a call to the center of the floor for all who wanted to participate in the salsa lessons. The thirty-minute session would be followed by live Latin music from a local band that had made a name for itself among the city's growing Latino community.

"Now, I know there are professionals here to teach you," Gabe said. "But you've got a pretty good salsa dancer sitting right here in front of you."

"*You're* going to teach me how to salsa?"

"My mother is from Honduras, remember? When I wasn't listening to 1960s Motown with my dad, I was dancing the salsa and punta with Mami." He held his hand out to her. "Now, let's see how well you listen to the teacher. Let's salsa."

Gabe took her through the steps of the rhythmic dance, his arousal heightening with every sensual shake of her hips.

"You're a quick learner, Mrs. Kirkland."

"Well, you're not my only teacher, Mr. Franklin. As you already pointed out, I got a head start watching *Dancing with the Stars*."

"Ah, that's right. You're starting ahead of the curve."

"So, how am I doing?" She stepped forward, twisting her waist and sticking her chest out.

Gabe leaned forward and brushed his lips against her neck. "Your body was born to salsa," he whispered against her skin.

He felt the slight shudder that rippled through her. An answering wave of desire coursed through him.

"Leslie," Gabe pushed out on a shaky breath.

"Is something wrong?"

"Hell no," he said. "Everything about this is right."

He glided his fingers along her arms. Her skin was damp from their dancing; the glistening softness matched what he'd dreamed she would feel like in his arms, hot and wet from making love. He wanted that so badly every molecule in his body ached with it, and every minute he spent feeling her move against him made him ache that much more.

By the time their dance lesson was over, Gabe was so aroused he was sure he would burst clear out of his skin. Sweet, pleasurable agony was the only way to describe what he was forced to endure for the next hour as he watched Leslie continue to dance to the beats of the live Latin band.

By the time they made it back to the car, Gabe was so wrung out he could barely walk. She reached over the center console and entwined her fingers with his.

"Thank you for tonight," she said. "I haven't had this much fun in so long. I forgot it was even possible."

"You already thanked me," he said. "Every time I saw you smiling and enjoying yourself, it was all the thanks I need."

"My goodness, you're sweet," she said on a rush of breath.

"Thank you." He brought her hand to his lips and kissed the crest of her fingers. "And you're welcome."

Her eyes narrowed in confusion. "For what?"

"For the kiss good-night you'll be thanking me for when I bring you home," he said with a wink.

Moments passed before she softly said, "Gabriel?"

"Yeah?" He started the car and put it in Drive.

"I don't want to tell you goodbye until the morning."

Gabe put the car in Park and shut off the engine.

He groaned, thumping his head back against the

headrest. "How can you tell me something like that when we still have an hour's drive ahead of us?"

"Sorry," she said, a hint of nervous amusement tinting her voice. "I probably should have kept it to myself until we made it home."

He squeezed his eyes tight and commanded his body find some control. It was a losing effort.

"If you knew how much I'm fighting the urge to lean that seat back and join you over there, you would probably run."

Her teasing laugh only heightened his arousal. "I'm not going anywhere but home with you."

He looked over at her, swallowed down the ball of lust that had instantly formed in his throat and asked, "Are you sure about this, Leslie? I don't want to pressure you into doing anything you're not ready to do. Don't think—"

She put two fingers up to his lips. "I'm sure," she said. "I'm ready to take this step, Gabriel. You make me *want* to take this step."

Gabe thought he would die of pleasure right then and there.

He started the car again and jerked the gearshift into Drive.

"This will be the longest damn ride of my life."

Leslie trailed a single finger along his jaw. "Just think about what will be waiting for you at the end of it."

He released another aching groan.

The next hour would be agony. Sweet, pleasurable agony.

With every mile the tires ate up on the road, Leslie tried to convince herself that she was ready for this. She was, dammit! She wanted this.

Of all the victories she'd celebrated on this journey of moving on with her life after losing Braylon, this one would be the most momentous. Giving her body to another man, sharing herself so intimately after all this time, was not something to take lightly. Leslie could not think of a single person she wanted to share this with more than the man sitting next to her.

She glanced over at Gabriel and studied his strong jaw. He had been quiet on the ride across Lake Pontchartrain, save for the deep, ragged breaths he would take ever so often. His grip on the steering wheel was so tight his knuckles were white.

"Are you okay?" Leslie asked.

He nodded. "Just trying not to blast through the speed limit on this damn bridge," he said.

"We have all night, Gabriel. The girls won't be home until morning."

"The night is more than halfway over," he said. He looked over at her, his eyes fiery with need. "If I knew this was how you planned for our night to end, you wouldn't have gotten salsa-dancing lessons."

She grinned. "I'm happy I didn't say anything until my lesson was over. I enjoyed dancing the salsa with you."

"It's so much better when you dance it naked. I'll show you how to do that, too."

She laughed, but the closer they got to Gauthier, the more her nervousness grew. By the time Gabriel turned into her driveway, Leslie was wound so tight her skin itched with it. Her anxiety must have shown on her face.

"Stop overthinking this," Gabriel said. "Nothing you said tonight is written in stone, Leslie. If you're not ready, then you're not ready."

She let out a shaky laugh. "You don't think I've made you wait long enough?"

"Have I complained?"

No, he hadn't. He had been so incredibly patient with her. For that reason alone she wanted to give herself to him.

He cupped her jaw and gently turned her to face him. "I'm not some horny teenager who's going to move on to the next girl if you decide you don't want to do this tonight. We don't have to. You're worth the wait, Leslie."

Instant heart melting.

He was the one who had been worth the wait. Leslie was convinced that she'd turned down all those dates with nice, sweet men this past year because she somehow knew *this* man was in her future. He was everything she had been looking for.

Yet her nerves still consumed her.

"It's been a long time since I did this, Gabriel," she admitted.

"I know," he said.

"And I've only done this with one man," she said.

He went still. The silence that entered the car was deafening.

"Don't let that freak you out," Leslie said.

"Your husband is the only man you've ever slept with? Ever?"

She pulled her bottom lip between her teeth and nodded. "I met Braylon when I was a freshman in college. He was the first boy I'd ever been with. And the last."

"Damn." He shook his head, his hands once again gripping the steering wheel. "And I'd always heard the girls who went to James Madison put out."

Her jaw dropped open. He looked over at her and

Leslie burst out laughing at the wicked grin creasing his face.

How could she be nervous about being with this sweet, kind, funny, gentle soul? Suddenly, Leslie couldn't think of anything she wanted to do more than release her body to him.

She slid her palm over his firm jaw and brushed her thumb over his lips. "Would you mind following me inside? I think it's time for you to reintroduced me to what I've been missing."

An irresistible grin tugged at the corner of his mouth. "It would be my pleasure."

They made it into the house in record time, kissing their way from the kitchen through the living room to the bedroom. Gabriel lifted her into his arms and lowered her onto the bed, trailing his mouth down her throat to the valley between her breasts.

"Lift up," he breathed against her skin. Leslie complied, sitting up so that he could unzip the hot-pink dress. He peeled it from her back and over her shoulders, then past her waist and down her legs, leaving her in her black satin panties and black pumps.

His desperate groan sent a hedonistic burst of pleasure ricocheting through her.

"I just need to look at you," he said.

"You just need to take your clothes off," Leslie returned.

That devilish grin returned. "My, aren't we eager?"

She lifted her leg and tapped at the center of his chest with her shoe. "I told you it's been a long time. I don't want to wait any longer."

His eyes instantly smoldered with heated need as he grabbed her leg and lifted it to his shoulder. He pressed a kiss to the inside of her ankle, then continued his way down, trailing his tongue along her leg and to her inner thigh. He flattened his palms on her legs and pushed them open. Then he dived for her center, nuzzling his mouth and nose against her dampening panties. He licked on either side of the strip of silky material before moving it to the side and brushing his lips against her exposed flesh.

Her body instantly melted with desire. Sensations swirled within her, tugging at her senses, teasing her brain with every delicate swipe of his tongue.

"More," Leslie whimpered, rolling her hips up and lifting herself to his face.

She felt Gabriel's breath flitter against her. "You asked for it," he whispered against her as he dragged the satin down her legs. He returned to the spot between her legs, spread her apart with his fingers and thrust his tongue inside.

Pleasure crashed through her.

He was relentless in his pursuit, stroking his tongue in and out while his finger toyed with the pulsing spot at her cleft, massaging it with increasing pressure. He moved his fingers aside and sucked the throbbing nub into his mouth, wrenching a scream out of her with every delicious tug.

She came with such force her entire body shook with it, yet Gabriel continued, his lips and teeth and tongue eliciting the most decadent sensations she had ever experienced. With one last, hard pull of his mouth, she shattered again, her body going limp with the ecstasy rioting through her.

Leslie's eyes fell closed as mind-bending pleasure washed over her.

"Give me just a minute," Gabriel said.

She managed to open her eyes long enough to see

him undressing. He unbuttoned the two top buttons of his shirt, then pulled it over his head, along with the undershirt beneath. He made quick work of unzipping his pants and pushing them and his briefs down in one quick motion.

Despite her orgasm-induced daze, Leslie was still conscious enough to recognize the sheer magnificence of his strong, compact body. He was all taut golden-brown skin over firm muscle.

He produced a condom from his wallet and rolled it over his stiff erection, then he climbed over her and went straight for the spot behind her ear. He teased the skin there, nipping and sucking, licking and biting. He slipped his hands underneath her and rolled her over, changing their position so that she was on top.

"That's better," Gabriel said. "This is the view I've been dreaming about." He glided his hands up her stomach and over her breasts, scraping his thumbnails across her nipples.

Leslie's stomach tightened in response.

"I can't wait any longer," she said. She reached between them and wrapped her fist around his thick erection. She lifted herself up slightly and, with her eyes falling closed, guided him into her.

Gabriel groaned. So did she.

With painstaking slowness she lowered herself onto his impressive length, her body opening around him, welcoming him inside. Leslie didn't move for several moments as she allowed her body to adjust to the sensation of being filled so completely.

It was breathtaking. His size, his strength, his understanding patience. She was so grateful it nearly drew tears to her eyes, but then Gabriel undulated his hips and she forgot about everything but the hot, engorged erection penetrating her body.

Leslie braced her hands on either side of his head and pumped up and down, rolling her hips with increasing fervor, squeezing around him with every plunge. Gabriel clamped his palms on her ass and pulled her down as he lifted up. The hard, deep thrust sent Leslie spiraling, another explosive orgasm tearing through her, leaving her spent and sated and gasping for breath.

"Oh, goodness," she said as she fell onto Gabriel's solid chest. She looked up at him, her mouth relaxing into a tired smile. "You, Mr. Franklin, were definitely worth the wait."

Chapter 10

Leslie burrowed herself deeper under the covers, her body seeking the unfamiliar warmth coming from the other side of the bed. It felt so good…yet…so…strange.

Her eyes popped open.

Her body stiffened. She wasn't alone.

For the first time in nearly two years, someone who wasn't Kristi during a thunderstorm was sharing her bed.

Leslie stared at the ornate chest of drawers that had been in this room since Braylon's parents had bought this house thirty years ago. As her eyes traced over the intricate carvings along the mahogany dresser's Queen Anne legs, she concentrated on controlling the numerous emotions rioting back and forth in her brain.

This wasn't a bad thing. It wasn't something she should be ashamed of. She was a young, healthy, normal woman. She should be able to enjoy spending the night with a man and not feeling as if her entire world would cave in on her in the morning. But that was exactly how she felt, as if the walls surrounding her would crumble at any second.

"Hey, are you awake?" Gabriel's groggy voice came from just over her shoulder.

Leslie went rigid, but after a few seconds forced herself to relax. She didn't want him to sense her anxiety over what they'd done last night. She didn't want to explain to him that none of what she was feeling right now was his fault.

"I am," she said.

Leslie felt his unbelievably soft lips on the center of her back. Her body warred with the urge to both flinch and liquefy with need. He had done so much for her last night. He'd reminded her of all the wonderful sensations she was capable of experiencing. The way he'd taken his time and worshipped her body was enough to make her melt this very second.

"I hate the thought of leaving you in bed like this," he said, moving his lips to her bare shoulder. "But I promised Tristan I'd help him out this morning. The high school band is preparing for the state competition."

"That's okay," Leslie said. "Shayla will be bringing the girls over soon anyway."

"Ah, yeah. That would be awkward. I'm not sure we're ready to explain this thing to Cassidy yet, are we?"

Leslie pushed out a breath. "Not just yet," she said. "Give me just a minute, then I'll let you have the bathroom."

She rose from the bed, trying her hardest not to feel self-conscious as she walked her naked body into the bathroom and grabbed the robe from behind the door.

Her hands fell still as she fingered Braylon's threadbare robe. The flimsy blue cotton was practically useless. She'd started wearing it during his first tour of duty, and even though he'd bought her several robes over the years, Leslie had never been able to make herself give up this one.

She could not bring herself to wear Braylon's robe while entertaining another man.

She pulled the one he'd bought her several Christmases ago from the bathroom closet. Leslie tried to quell the nausea building in her belly as she threaded her arms through the satin robe and tied the sash tight at her waist.

When she exited the bathroom Gabriel was standing on the other side of the bed, his pants on but unzipped.

"Oh, I'm sorry," Leslie said.

He looked up at her, his brow cocked in an amused expression. "It would be a little late for me to be modest, wouldn't it?"

Her cheeks heated as she shook her head. "I guess so." Her voice cracked on the last word.

Gabriel tilted his head to the side, his steady gaze roaming over her face. "Leslie, is something wrong?"

She watched him as he slid his arms through the sleeves of his shirt and pulled it over his head.

"No, nothing," she lied. "Do you...uh...do you want some coffee?"

He came to where she stood and wrapped his arms around her waist, lacing his fingers at the small of her back. "I wish I could stay for coffee, but I should have been at the high school ten minutes ago. I'm going to run over to my place to shower and change."

He dipped his head, captured her lips in a slow, deep kiss. Leslie tried to enjoy it, but just before her eyes would have fallen closed, she glanced at the nightstand and saw the picture of Braylon in his uniform. The sickening feeling that had been threatening to overtake her flooded her gut.

She pulled her head back and pushed at Gabriel's chest.

"I need you to go," she said, her voice hoarse, her throat suddenly aching.

The disappointment that immediately clouded Gabriel's face was too much for her to handle right now.

He took a step forward. She stepped back.

"Come on, Leslie, don't do this," he said, reaching for her.

Leslie sidestepped him and walked swiftly out of the room, heading for the kitchen. She had the door opened by the time Gabriel made it to the room.

"I'm so sorry," she said. "I just can't deal with…with this right now. I need some time. Please just leave."

"Leslie." Her name came out on a painful sigh. "Let me help you through this. We can talk it out, but you can't push me away."

He reached for her again, but she twisted away from his touch.

"Gabriel, please," she said much louder than she'd intended.

His hands fell to his sides. The look on his face was one of pure agony. But she couldn't be concerned with his pain right now. Not when her own was threatening to suffocate her.

Without another word he grabbed his keys from the table and walked out. He stopped on the second step and turned back to look at her. The heartbreak in his eyes stole the breath from her lungs. Time stood still as their gazes locked across the mere feet that separated them. It could have very well been miles.

Gabriel shook his head, shoved his hands into his pockets and continued down the steps, never once looking back as he got into his car and backed out of the driveway.

The minute Leslie closed the door, she dropped her head against it and tears started to stream down her face.

"Damn you, Braylon," she choked out. Then, with enough force to shake the walls, she screamed, *"Damn you!"*

She tore out of the kitchen, ran to the bedroom and grabbed the photograph from her nightstand.

"Look what you did to me!" she yelled at her dead husband's face. "Look what I've become! A damn coward who's too afraid to let a good man love me.

"Damn you!" she screamed again and hurled the picture at the wall.

The crash of the glass resonated through the room as it broke into pieces. Leslie crumbled onto the hardwood floor and rolled into a ball, her body racked with sobs. She folded her arms over her stomach and cried until she had nothing left.

"Dude? What the hell?"

Gabe looked over his shoulder and spotted Tristan standing on the other side of the chain-link fence. Ignoring him, Gabe dribbled the basketball a couple of times before taking a shot. He missed. Again.

"Is this what you call helping me? Practicing your weak-ass jump shot?"

"Not the time," Gabe said as he set up for another

shot. The ball rolled around the rim before falling…on the outside of the net.

Dammit. But based on the rest of his morning, that was par for the course.

He shot the ball up again, banging it hard off the backboard and right into Tristan's hands.

"You want to give that to me?" Gabe asked.

"Nah," Tristan said, tucking the ball under his arm. He nodded toward Gabe's chest. "You run out of clean basketball gear?"

Gabe looked down at his clothes. His once crisply ironed white shirt was now wrinkled and damp from the sweat he'd worked up running around on the basketball court for the past hour, and dancing the salsa at the Blue Nile last night. His pants weren't in much better shape, and he didn't want to think about the beating his shoes had taken on the unforgiving asphalt.

"Look, I'm sorry I never showed up to help out with the band. I've got a lot on my mind. Can you just give me my ball and let me hang out here alone for a while?"

"How long have you known me?" Tristan asked.

Gabe didn't answer. It wasn't as if Tristan needed one.

His friend continued, "And in all that time, when have you known me to leave you moping?"

"I'm not moping." Gabe reached for the ball. The bastard switched arms.

"Oh, you are moping, my friend." Tristan dribbled the ball a couple of times, then tried unsuccessfully to spin it on his fingertip. "Does your current mood have anything to do with a pretty widow that likes to volunteer in your class?"

Gabe's mouth dropped open.

"Oh, come on," Tristan said. "Seriously, man, how

long have you known me? You think I didn't see this
coming a mile away?"

"But we've been careful as hell," Gabe said. "No one
was supposed to know."

Pain sliced through his chest the moment the words
left his mouth.

He should have known this thing between them was
doomed from the minute she'd insisted they keep it
quiet. She never would have been comfortable enough
to bring their relationship out into the open.

"I don't know if anyone else figured it out," Tristan
said. "Then again, I don't know if anyone else pays
close enough attention to you to recognize how different you've been lately."

Gabe's head reared back. "How have I been different?"

"You've been happy. Less stressed." Tristan dribbled
the ball a couple more times, then tossed it to Gabe.
"I'm guessing something that falls into the not-so-good
category happened last night, otherwise you wouldn't
be out here playing basketball in your Sunday best."

"Actually, what happened last night falls into the
best-night-of-my-life category. It was this morning
when everything went to hell." Gabe let the ball fall
from his hands without taking a shot. "I don't know
what went wrong. No. I *do* know what went wrong.
We moved too fast, and she wasn't ready to handle it."

"You had to have known that it would be tricky dating someone with the kind of baggage Leslie Kirkland
carries. Or did you not know about her baggage?"

"I knew her husband died."

"Do you know *how* he died?"

Gabe nodded. "She told me the first time we went
out. But he died two years ago. I thought—hoped—that

it was enough time for her to have worked through her issues over it. Apparently, I was wrong."

Tristan picked up the ball and took a shot, sinking it through the net.

"So, what now?" he asked.

"What in the hell do you think I've been trying to figure out here on this basketball court?" Gabe asked, taking the ball and trying again. He missed, but caught his own rebound.

"You come up with anything good?" Tristan asked.

"There's only one thing I can do," Gabe said. He looked over at his old roommate and shook his head. "I can't accept any other alternative."

He tossed the ball to Tristan and then took off for his car.

Chapter 11

Leslie didn't know how much time had passed when she heard knocking at the kitchen door. She tried to lift herself up, but she was too weak to move, her body still wrung out from the deluge of anguish that had overtaken her. A minute later she heard the kitchen door open and Shayla calling her name.

"Les? Are you here?"

Moments later her bedroom door creaked opened. She heard Shayla gasp, and in a heartbeat her sister-in-law was at her side.

"Oh, my God, Leslie! What happened? Are you hurt?"

"I'm okay," Leslie said, pushing herself up before Shayla called 911.

"What happened?" Shayla asked again. Her eyes darted from Leslie to the shattered picture frame. Understanding washed over her face. "Oh, Les," she said.

"Mom?" Cassidy called, followed by Buster's squeaky bark.

Shayla quickly pushed herself up from the floor. "Don't worry, I've got them," she said before backing out of the room.

Leslie didn't put up an argument. She felt too broken to do anything.

Five minutes later, Shayla came back into the room. Leslie was exactly where she'd left her.

"Oh, honey," Shayla said. She walked over and sat on the floor next to her.

Leslie tried to keep the tears at bay, but it was as if she'd released the hinges on a dam that had been closed for too many years. The force of the tide was too strong to stop it. She cried until her body ached with it, until she was too weak to do anything more than rest in Shayla's arms.

"It's okay," Shayla murmured as she ran a soothing hand over Leslie's head again and again. "It's going to be okay, honey. It's going to be okay."

"When?" The single word came out hoarse and craggy. "When will it be okay, Shayla? It's been two years and nothing is okay."

Leslie wiped her nose on the sleeve of her robe and looked up at her sister-in-law. She and Braylon had the same deep brown eyes, the same eyes that her daughters had.

"It's not okay. I slept with Gabriel," Leslie admitted in a small voice. "In this room. I slept with another man in my husband's bed."

"Oh, honey, don't. Don't you dare do this to yourself," Shayla said. She cradled Leslie in her arms again, rocking from side to side as guilty tears once again overwhelmed her. "This is exactly where you should have slept with Gabriel, because this is *your* room, not Braylon's. This is healthy, Leslie. This is right."

"Taking another man to my husband's bed is right?"

"You're damn right it's right," Shayla said. "You told me yourself that you and Braylon talked about this. This is what he wanted for you if anything ever happened to him. There's no reason to be angry with yourself for doing something that Braylon would have wanted. I mean it, Leslie. Don't you dare feel one ounce of guilt about sleeping with Gabriel."

Shayla lifted Leslie's chin so that she could look her in the eyes.

"Is it really you that you're angry with?" she asked. "Or is it Braylon?"

Leslie pulled her trembling bottom lip between her teeth. "It's Braylon," Shayla stated. "He's the one you're angry with."

She nodded, the tears once again cascading down her cheeks.

"I am," Leslie admitted. "God, I am still *so* angry with him," she said. "Why, Shayla? Why did he do it? I thought I'd dealt with all of this, but I need to ask him why. Why didn't he come to me and let me help him? Why did he leave me to raise these girls on my own?"

Shayla smoothed Leslie's hair away from her face, her own eyes brimming with tears.

"You're never going to get those answers, sweetheart. I wish that you could—God, do I wish you could—but you need to accept that you won't. Braylon is gone. He's not coming back. You have to figure out a way to get past this, Les."

"I know," she said. She sniffed. "I've…I've been planning to ask for a transfer…to the Houston office. I thought maybe getting away from Gauthier would help."

Leslie felt Shayla stiffen. She heard her swallow. "Moving?"

"I know it's selfish, but sometimes I hate walking into this house, Shayla. Dealing with the memories. It's just so hard."

"Do you really think moving will help, though? You can't run away from this, Leslie."

"I know," Leslie whispered.

Shayla tipped her chin up again. "Whatever you choose to do, you need to make sure that it helps you to really work through these issues, honey. If that means moving, then I guess you have to do what you have to do. But I really think you need to talk to someone, a professional who can help you through this."

Leslie nodded.

"You have a life ahead of you, Les. You have two beautiful daughters. You have family that loves you and who is willing to do anything for you. Anything."

"Thank you," Leslie said. "I don't know how I would have gotten through these two years without you, Shayla."

"You would have, because you're strong. You're so much stronger than you give yourself credit for. But you never have to worry about getting through anything alone. Remember that."

Shayla cradled Leslie's face in her palms. "I need you to do something for me," she said. "Before you make any decisions about leaving, I need you to think about the future you want for yourself."

"I have been thinking about the future," Leslie said.

"And do you see Gabriel in that future?"

"I can," Leslie said. "I *do*. But I'm afraid I ran him off."

"If he's the man I think he is, he'll be back," Shayla said.

Leslie's reply to that was an exhausted sigh. She remained on the floor with Shayla, allowing herself to be held. She was so tired of being strong, so tired of putting on that brave front that was nothing but a facade, despite what her sister-in-law thought.

"Where are the girls and Buster?" she whispered after some time had passed.

"I walked them over to Gayle's next door. She was working in her garden. She said she would watch them for however long I needed. Do you want me to go get them?"

The floorboards let out a loud creak, drawing both Shayla's and Leslie's attention to the bedroom doorway. Gabriel stood just outside the room, his hands shoved into the pockets of the pants he'd worn last night.

"Actually," Shayla said, "why don't I take the girls out for ice cream?"

"Thanks," Leslie said, her voice still hoarse from her tears.

"It's what aunties are for, right?" Shayla smiled at Gabriel as she eased past him. A few seconds later, the kitchen door banged shut.

The awkward silence that followed Shayla's departure scratched at Leslie's skin. With a heavy exhale she pushed herself up from the floor. "Can you give me a minute to get dressed?" she asked.

He nodded but didn't speak.

Leslie fled to the safety of her bathroom, shutting the door behind her and leaning back on it. Her eyes slid shut as she stood there for a moment and concentrated on taking deep, cleansing breaths. She walked over to the sink and gripped the edges.

Staring at the face looking back at her, she hardly recognized the woman in the mirror. She looked the same, yet everything was completely different. She *was* different. She was *strong.*

She'd endured immeasurable pain, yet she was still standing, just as Shayla had told her. Just as the man on the other side of the door had told her.

That man on the other side of the door was her future.

That was, if she hadn't already pushed him away. But if she had pushed him away, would he be here?

Hope replacing some of the pain in her chest, Leslie turned on the faucet and washed the remnants of the past tearful hours from her face. She slipped on the white sundress with eyelet trim that she liked to wear around the house and ran a brush through her hair. When she opened the door, Gabriel was sitting on the Queen Anne chair she kept in the corner next to the cheval mirror. He rose when she emerged from the bathroom, but he still didn't speak.

"I'm sorry," Leslie opened. She shook her head, knowing the words were inadequate. "It was unfair of me to throw you out the way I did."

"I just want to know what happened, Leslie."

She pulled her trembling bottom lip between her teeth, and Gabriel's face crumbled.

"Please, don't cry," he said, coming toward her. He wrapped his arms around her and cradled her against his chest. "Don't cry. I don't want to upset you. I just want to know what I did wrong. Did I push too hard? Did I pressure you?"

"No!" She shook her head. "You didn't pressure me into doing anything I didn't want to do. You didn't do anything wrong, Gabriel." She pulled back and swiped at her cheeks. "Neither did I. Neither of us did anything wrong."

"So what was that about this morning?" he asked, his voice filled with painful confusion.

"I never expected the guilt I would feel the first time I brought another man into this house."

"Aw, baby." He cupped the back of her head and held her to him. "I didn't even think about how that would affect you. I'm sorry."

"You have nothing to be sorry about. It was time for this to happen, Gabriel. All of it. I've cried so much today that I'm surprised I have any tears left, but it's what I needed." She looked up from where she lay against his chest. "Do you know the last time I allowed myself to cry like this? The day of Braylon's funeral. Sure, I've cried, but I never just let it all out like this, and *never* in front of anyone. Ever. Whenever I felt myself getting too emotional, I would do everything I could to stop it."

"Leslie—"

"I had survived deployment after deployment and heard on a constant basis how brave I was in the face of all that stress. People expected me to be strong. They didn't expect tears."

"You lost your husband. You lost him in one of the most tragic ways imaginable. No one could expect you to stay strong through that."

She pointed to her chest. "*I* did. And I was. I was so strong throughout all of it. But, goodness, Gabriel, I couldn't be strong anymore. I needed to let myself feel.

"What we did last night was the biggest step I've taken in letting go of Braylon. I've shied away from dating because I've been so afraid to take that step. I've been unsure of what it would mean, unsure if it meant that I would have to completely close that chapter of my life. But I'm ready to move on. Truly ready," she said. "And if you're still willing, I really want to move on with you."

He captured her shoulders and dipped his head until he'd caught her gaze.

"You have to promise me something."

"Anything."

"I mean it, Leslie. Promise me you won't send me away the next time you feel yourself falling apart. I'm not naive. I know that this will happen again. But you have to let me be there for you when it does." He gently caressed her cheek with the backs of his fingers. "If we're going to be together, you have to trust me with every part of you, especially your heart."

She closed her eyes and let her head fall forward onto his chest.

"I trust you," she whispered. "And I promise never to shut you out like that again."

He lifted her head and stared into her eyes, his soulful gaze reaching the very heart of her.

"In that case, there is nothing else I'd rather do in life than embark on this brand-new future with you."

Leslie shielded her eyes against the bright sun peeking through the thick branches of the oaks that resided in Heritage Park, the landmark that divided the east and west sides of Gauthier's Main Street. The park, like the rest of Main Street, had undergone a resurgence in the past few years. The growth was fueled by the local civic association's drive to rebrand Gauthier as a tourist destination. If the flood of people who flocked to downtown Gauthier on the weekends—shopping, eating at Emile's Restaurant or enjoying a cappuccino on the sidewalk seating in front of The Jazzy Bean—was any indication, the rebranding effort had been a success.

Heritage Park had undergone the biggest transformation, being restored to its former glory, with its wooden waterwheel—the focal point of the park—once again churning. This past fall, local attorney and state representative Matthew Gauthier, whose family founded the town, led an effort to make Heritage Park more kid-friendly. An overgrown area of trees and brush had been cleared away and brand-new playground equipment had been brought in.

"Mama, watch this!" Kristi called.

Still shielding her eyes, Leslie looked on as Kristi climbed up the rungs of the *big-girl slide*. When she made it to the top, she waved down at Leslie, then turned around with her back to the slide, preparing to slide backward.

"Kristi!" Leslie called, taking off for the slide. "Don't you dare!"

Kristi turned and started to howl with laughter. "I'm just joking, Mom! Cassidy told me you would have a heart attack if I did that."

Leslie plunked her hands on her hips. "Is that what you want? You want to give your mother a heart attack?"

Kristi hunched her shoulders. "I don't know. What is a heart attack, anyway?"

Leslie heard laughter coming from behind her. She turned and spotted Shayla a couple of yards away.

"You'll find out if you try that again," Shayla called to Kristi. "You're going to give both me and your mom a heart attack."

"Slide down the right way or don't slide at all," Leslie told her daughter. She turned to Shayla. "These children will be the death of me."

"You and me both," Shayla said. Her lips dipped in a sad smile. "How are you doing?"

"Better," Leslie said with a nod. "Definitely better than the last time you saw me."

"Did you and Gabriel talk?"

"Yes. And, before I say anything else, let me reassure you that the girls and I are not leaving Gauthier."

Shayla brought her hands to her mouth, instant tears springing to the corners of her eyes.

"Thank God," she said. "Xavier was ready to write me a prescription for anxiety meds. I've been a mess since yesterday."

"Honey, I am so sorry I worried you."

Shayla shook her head and wiped at the tears that had escaped. "I can't tell you what to do with the girls. But I just got them, Les. It's my own fault for staying away for so long, but now that they are in my life I cannot imagine not having them there. I told Xavier last night that we would have to look for a house in Houston. It was just that simple."

Gratitude pumped through Leslie's veins at her words. To know that her sister-in-law was willing to go to such lengths to stay in Kristi's and Cass's lives meant everything.

"You don't have to worry about that," Leslie said. "We're not going anywhere anytime soon. Well, except for the beach."

Shayla's eyes widened. "The beach?"

"Gabriel asked me and the girls to join him at a beach house he rented in Biloxi. He's bringing his siblings out for spring break."

"You're going to the beach in Biloxi?" Trepidation colored Shayla's voice. "Does Gabriel know that's where Braylon killed himself?"

Leslie shook her head. "I haven't told him."

"Are you sure you're ready to handle this, Les?"

"Last night, after you left—after Gabriel left—I had a long talk with Braylon. I told him I loved him." She took a deep breath. "But that I had to leave him behind. So, yes," she said with a vigorous nod. "I'm ready to handle the beach. I'm ready to start making new memories with the man that I love. And where better to start making them?"

"Oh, honey," Shayla said, enveloping her in a hug. "You are the very definition of incredible. I'm so proud of you."

"Thank you," Leslie said. She laughed. "Now all I have to do is figure out how to tell my daughter that I'm dating her teacher."

Shayla laughed. "Good luck with that. You never know. She may think it's cool."

Leslie was astounded to discover that Shayla was right. After they left the park, Leslie took the girls on a stroll around the neighborhood so that Buster could get some exercise. As Cassidy struggled to get the stubborn dog out of Mrs. Black's prized blue-eyed daisies, Leslie brought up the subject of Gabriel.

"Cass, you've noticed how Mr. Franklin has been coming over to the house, haven't you?"

"Yeah," Cassidy said. "Get out of there, Buster! Why is this dog so stupid?"

"Stop calling Buster stupid," Kristi protested. "You're stupid."

"Kristi," Leslie admonished.

"She called Buster stupid, but Buster can't say it back, so I said it for her."

Leslie didn't know how to defend herself against that logic. She wouldn't even try.

"As I was saying," she continued. "Mr. Franklin has been coming around lately because we've been seeing each other."

"You're Mr. Franklin's girlfriend?" Cassidy asked.

Leslie's breath stilled in her lungs. Apprehension skirted down her spine as she nodded. "Yes," she said. "I'm his girlfriend. Are you okay with that?"

Cassidy tilted her head to the side, then shrugged. "Sure. You needed a boyfriend."

Leslie's jaw dropped. "Excuse me?"

"Mom's got a boyfriend," Kristi sang, shaking her hips. "Mom and her boyfriend sittin' in a tree...*k-i-s*... What's the rest?"

Cassidy rolled her eyes.

Leslie looked between her two girls and burst out laughing. "You two never cease to surprise me. Come on, let's get Buster home. The two of you are giving her a bath."

Kristi and Cassidy both groaned.

Leslie used the ace she kept in her pocket, a bacon-flavored dog treat, to cajole Buster away from the daisies. As they turned onto Collins, they encountered Sawyer Robertson jogging up the street.

"Well, hello," he said, his entire body drenched in perspiration.

"Hello, Sawyer," Leslie greeted.

"Guess what?" Kristi said. *Oh, no.* "My mom has a boyfriend. He's Cass's teacher."

Oh, Lord. Leslie's eyes went wide.

"Really?" Sawyer said, crossing his arms over his chest. He looked at Leslie. "Congratulations. Maybe now the deaconesses will lay off. I was a real disappointment to them when it came to snagging your attention."

Leslie shook her head, a mixture of chagrin and relief washing through her. "I knew it," she said. "Those meddling women. I'm so sorry for anything they said to you."

"It's okay," Sawyer said. "If I was at another time in my life, I would give that new boyfriend of yours a run for his money." He winked, then waved at the girls before continuing along the sidewalk.

Leslie watched him jog away, thinking that one day that man would definitely make some lucky lady very happy.

Chapter 12

Leslie snuggled closer into the cocoon Gabriel's body created around her. She rested her head on his firm biceps as they rocked slowly from side to side, watching the volleyball game taking place just down the beach.

Gabriel's younger brother, Elias, held Kristi up on his neck so she would be tall enough to hit the ball over the net. Cassidy was busy trying to impress her new idol, Daniela, by diving for each and every ball that came her way.

Even though dusk would be upon them soon, Leslie didn't want to stop the game until she absolutely had to. It was their last night at the beach house, and she wanted the kids to soak in as much fun as they could. Besides, she was perfectly fine where she was, her bottom settled in the sand, her back resting against Gabriel's solid chest. She could feel his heartbeats, the steady rhythm lulling her into a state of such contentment. She could stay right here forever.

Leslie had been cautious about her and Gabriel being too affectionate around the girls, even choosing to sleep in the room with Kristi and Cassidy their first two nights at the beach house. Then, yesterday, Cass had come up to her while she was packing their picnic lunch and told Leslie that she and Mr. Franklin sure didn't act like girlfriend and boyfriend. It was then that Leslie decided her girls would probably be okay with seeing a little affection between her and Gabriel.

And she was ever so grateful, especially after spending last night in bed with him. He'd spent hours showing her just how affectionate he could be. It had continued throughout today. Now that they'd given themselves permission to be more open about their relationship around the kids, Gabriel didn't hesitate to show it.

During the past hour as they'd sat wrapped in each other's arms out on the beach, Leslie had grown used to his featherlight kisses along her cheek, down the slope of her neck, on her bare shoulder.

He tightened his arms around her and pressed a kiss to her temple. "You still doing okay?"

She rolled her eyes and let out a sigh. "For the hundredth time, yes, Mr. Worrywart."

"You can be as sassy as you want to, smart-ass. Still won't stop me from asking."

Leslie had decided to wait until they'd arrived at the rented beach house before giving Gabriel the full details of Braylon's suicide. She'd told him about the trip she, Braylon and the girls had taken two years ago to the beach in Biloxi, and how the day after they'd gotten back home, Braylon had returned to Mississippi, parked on the beach and shot himself in the head.

Just as she'd anticipated, Gabriel had been horrified that he'd brought her to this place that had such awful memories. He'd insisted they leave immediately, but Leslie had refused. And she was happy she hadn't let him talk her into returning to Gauthier.

She'd found peace again on this beach.

Coming back to the place where Braylon had taken his life, confronting the memories it held and accepting that it was okay to move on had been the true start of her healing process. It felt as if every burden she'd carried for the past two years had lifted from her shoulders. She was ready to face her future. Knowing the man whose strong arms surrounded her would be a part of that future brought her peace so immense that Leslie couldn't put it into words.

But words were unnecessary. All it took was one look, one faint caress of his fingers along her skin, one gentle press of his soft, sweet lips against her own. And there it was. Peace.

"Do you think we can get them away from that volleyball game?" he asked.

"It'll be difficult, but I think I know one way," Leslie said. She pushed up from the sand and walked over to the volleyball net.

"Who wants to roast marshmallows?" she called.

The volleyball game was instantly forgotten.

Ten minutes later they all were seated around the beach house's built-in fire pit. Kristi squealed every time the orange flame licked her giant marshmallow.

"This needs chocolate and graham crackers," Daniela said.

"Oh, s'mores! That would have been so good." Leslie playfully elbowed Gabriel in the rib cage. "Why didn't you think of that?"

"Sorry," he said. "Maybe next time."

The thought of a next time sent a spiral of pleasure

through Leslie's bloodstream. "Definitely next time," she said.

The sun had just begun its descent into the calm gulf waters when Gabriel's cell phone rang. He slipped it out of his pocket and answered.

"Hey, Tristan, what's up?"

His brow creased in concern, setting Leslie instantly on edge.

"What the hell?" Gabriel said. He jumped up from the Adirondack chair. "Ask Matt to stall for as long as he can. I'll be there as soon as possible."

Leslie stood, her heart in her throat.

Gabriel looked at her, his expression a mixture of fury and disbelief. "We need to get back to Gauthier right now."

The normally hour-and-a-half drive from Biloxi took them almost two hours due to spring-break traffic heading from the many beachfront properties. Gabe had filled Leslie in on his short phone call with Tristan.

Before they'd crossed the Mississippi State line, Tristan had already called twice more, relaying what was taking place at the emergency meeting that had been called after word broke that the school board had convened in a hastily called Sunday-afternoon board meeting and decided that Gauthier Elementary and Middle School should be closed and all students moved to the new facility on Highway 421.

Gabe banged his fist on the steering wheel.

"Tristan told me this would happen. You told me this would happen. Hell, everybody told me this would happen."

"It hasn't happened yet," Leslie said. "Let's just get to the school."

When they pulled up to GEMS, there were so many cars that Gabe had to park along the highway.

Leslie had called Shayla when they were still ten minutes out. She spotted her sister-in-law waiting outside the doors of the school auditorium. Shayla wrapped an arm around Cass's shoulders and the other around Kristi's and asked the girls if they were up for a late-night movie. She invited Daniela and Elias to come along, as well.

Leslie gave her a grateful kiss on the cheek before hurrying into the auditorium.

The place looked to be on the brink of pandemonium. Angry parents barked at the superintendent and other school-board members, while Matt Gauthier and his wife, Tamryn, implored people to get in line and use the two microphones that had been set up on either side of the auditorium.

Leslie rushed to the nearest microphone.

"Quiet down, everyone," she called. "Please, quiet down."

Well, that didn't work.

Leslie spotted a gavel on the table where the school-board members sat. She grabbed the gavel, brought it to the microphone and banged with all her might. That got their attention.

"People, *please*," Leslie said. "We all know that screaming won't get us anywhere."

"I told you they were gonna close the school," Janice yelled. "I told you!"

"Has the school board explained their position?" Leslie asked.

"Not yet," Matt Gauthier said. "I think we should all quiet down and give them the chance to do just that."

Matt turned to the seated board. "Superintendent Mc-Cabe, the floor is yours."

The head of the school board stood and buttoned his suit coat. He walked over to the microphone on the other side of the auditorium and began.

"After much consideration, the board has come to the conclusion that it is in the financial best interest of the parish school system that both the elementary and middle-school portions of GEMS join with Maplesville Middle School."

"What about the merger? Wasn't it supposed to be just the middle school?" a parent asked.

"The merger was originally part of a pilot study being funded by the Department of Education, but the DOE has decided to postpone its rollout of the program for another two years. However, the board believes it is in the best interest of the parish that the merger still take place."

"What about the best interest of our children?"

"And what about the teachers? Will they all still have their jobs?"

McCabe held his hands up. "The majority of the teachers will retain their positions, although there may be a few who will have to move to other schools within the parish."

"This is a big parish," Matt pointed out. "That can mean a long drive for some, depending on where they are placed."

The superintendent hunched his shoulders in an "it's the best I can do" gesture.

"What about Principal Williams? Will he still move to the new school?" came another question from a parent.

"Technically, it will not be a new school," the superintendent said. "Only a new building. Thus, Principal Grayson at Maplesville Middle will retain his principalship over the school. The board is recommending Principal Williams for early retirement."

There was a collective gasp followed by a torrent of angry outbursts directed at the school-board members. It took another three minutes before they were able to quiet the crowd again. Superintendent McCabe continued with the justification for closing GEMS, spouting numbers and explaining how the money saved would benefit the town of Gauthier in other areas.

No one in the room was buying it. They all knew that whatever money was saved would be filtered into the more densely populated cities within the parish. They'd been through this before.

Leslie looked over at Gabriel, who had been quiet since entering the auditorium. He stood with his arms crossed over his chest, his jaw so hard it looked like granite.

"What about the other administrative positions?" Leslie asked McCabe. "The secretary, school counselor." She glanced at Gabriel again. "The assistant principal."

Gabriel turned and locked eyes with her.

"The other positions are safe," the superintendent said. "The larger student population will warrant an additional secretary, counselor and librarian. And a school that size warrants two assistant principals, so Mr. Franklin would move into a permanent assistant principal position there."

"I don't want it," Gabriel stated.

Leslie's eyes widened at his cold, direct statement. He turned his attention to the school board as he made his way to the microphone. Leslie stepped aside so that he could speak.

"I was offered a permanent assistant principal position at Gauthier Elementary and Middle School, not Maplesville Middle School. I made promises to the people of this community based on information you provided, Superintendent McCabe. Those promises I made have turned out to be lies, and I won't allow you to stand here and make a liar of me."

Leslie wanted to yank the mic away from his mouth. Being insubordinate to the board in front of the entire town was one way to guarantee that he would never get that assistant principal position. It meant too much to him—too much *for* him and his entire family—to jeopardize it.

At the same time, she wanted to wrap her arms around him in front of the entire world. She wanted to show everyone just how much she loved this strong, brave man who would risk so much for his convictions. Her heart felt on the verge of bursting with love and pride as he continued his denouncement of the school board's decision.

"The people of Gauthier will not stand for this," Gabriel said. "And I plan to be the first one on the front lines as we fight to keep this school open."

The crowd, who just weeks ago had ranted at him, now stood and cheered.

Matt Gauthier leaned over to the microphone. "And I'll serve as legal counsel for the parents of GEMS," he said, eliciting more cheers.

Another of the school-board members made it to the microphone where Superintendent McCabe stood, his neck as red as a fire hydrant.

"Nothing the superintendent has discussed is set in

stone," the board member said. "These are all just rec-
ommendations. There is still much discussion that will
go on before final decisions are made."

"I know you all just got voted back into office, but
there is this thing known as a recall," Janice Taylor
said. "If any of you want to keep your positions on the
school board, you'd better make sure one of those decisions is that this school stays open. I don't make empty
threats. I will work day and night to make sure none of
you ever serves on a school board again."

Janice's impassioned proclamation riled the crowd
up again, but Leslie didn't bother to quiet them. Everything that needed to be said had been said.

Instead, she grabbed Gabriel's wrist and tugged him
to her. Then wrapped her arms around his neck and
kissed him square on the mouth in front of everyone.
Although, it wasn't as if anyone was paying attention
to them.

"Do you know what you just did?" she asked him.

"Do you know what *you* just did?" he asked, motioning around them.

"I don't care who sees us together, Gabriel. I want
everyone to see us together."

His eyes softened, love and gratitude beaming in
their brown depths. He linked their fingers together
and urged her to follow him. They stepped out a side
door and into a slim corridor just off to the right of the
auditorium.

"As much as I love the thought of you ravishing me in
front of the entire town, it was too damn loud in there."

Leslie laughed, linking her arms around his neck
and pulling his mouth to hers again. The kiss was swift
but deep, tinged with the promise that there would be
more to come later. But right now they needed to talk.

"Gabriel, I'm concerned about you," she said. "About your future. You do realize that you can kiss that assistant principal position goodbye, don't you? Even if they do keep the school open, McCabe will find a way to make you pay for what you did tonight."

"You don't have to worry about me," he said. "No matter what happens, I'll be okay. So will Mami, Daniela and Elias. I'll find a way to make it work." He enclosed her in his arms, linked his fingers at the small of her back and pulled her in until she was flush against him. "As for my future, as long as you're in it, nothing else matters."

Leslie's heart melted then and there.

"I mean it, Leslie," he whispered against her lips. "None of that other stuff matters. All I want is to be forever with you."

Epilogue

Three months later

"**D**id you remember to pick up the chocolate bars?" Leslie asked as she scooted up behind Gabriel and slid her palms over his stomach.

He covered her arms and turned his head, catching her lips in a quick kiss.

"Yes, I remembered the chocolate bars and graham crackers and bought an extra bag of marshmallows just in case."

"Always going above and beyond. I'll bet you were the teacher's pet in school."

"I was the teacher's headache," he said with a deep chuckle. "I'm trying to make up for being such a troublemaker all those years ago."

Just then a sandy volleyball bounced off the side of his head.

"Hey!" Gabriel yelled.

"Sorry, bro," Elias called. Kristi was laughing so hard she fell to her knees in the sand. Buster, as usual, danced around her like the party had just gotten started.

Elias jogged over to where Leslie and Gabriel sat in the sand.

"Sorry," he said again, picking up the ball from where it had rolled after clunking Gabriel upside the head. The handsome teenager had a smile so much like his older brother's. Leslie knew he would drive the girls around Gauthier High School wild when he started there in just a few weeks.

Elias was the one who had suggested moving to Louisiana to live with Gabriel instead of transferring to an expensive private school in Houston. As he'd pointed out to Gabriel, changing schools wouldn't mean all that much if he was going to remain in that same neighborhood. Elias wanted to make a clean break. Leslie could not have been more supportive of the decision to bring him here.

"Is Cass still upset that Daniela didn't come to the beach house?" Leslie asked, scooting around so that she now faced him.

"She remembers to pout every now and again," Gabe said. "But then she starts having fun and forgets. Daniela doesn't. I've gotten at least a dozen texts from her since we've been here, bellyaching about missing out on the fun. She says it's unfair that she's stuck in the middle of nowhere."

"She's not in the middle of nowhere. She's in Lubbock."

His brow arched. "Have you ever been to Lubbock? Believe me, it's the middle of nowhere. But she's the one who wanted to get a head start on school."

Leslie playfully bumped his leg. "Admit it, you're proud of her."

"Yeah, I am," he said. "I hate that she's missing out on this, though."

"I do, too. Maybe we can rent this place again in the spring, and she can come for spring break."

"Rent? I think we should just buy it. We can afford it. You know, with all the extra money I'll be making."

It had not taken the school-board members long to reverse their opinion on closing GEMS. Gabriel was named the permanent assistant principal soon after, and it was announced that the new building, which was initially slated to be the new site of Maplesville High School, would fulfill its original purpose.

"So, that assistant principal position pays *that* much?" Leslie asked.

A rueful grin stretched across his face. "Okay, so maybe we can buy that shack at the far end of the beach."

With a laugh, Leslie said, "For you, I would live in a shack, but I just cut my commute in half a few months ago. Don't make me drive all the way from Biloxi to the satellite office in Maplesville everyday."

"Okay, okay. No beach house," Gabriel said. He hooked his arms under her knees and leaned forward, pressing a kiss to her lips. "I guess we'll make do with that pretty little house in Gauthier, *amor.*"

"Are you sure that's enough for you?"

"Absolutely." He smiled into her eyes. "As long as you're there, that's all I'll ever need."

* * * * *

Don't miss Farrah Rochon's next BAYOU DREAMS romance, STAY WITH ME FOREVER, available August 2015 from Harlequin Kimani Romance!

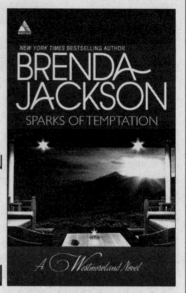

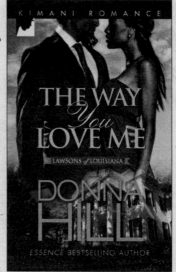

REQUEST YOUR FREE BOOKS!

2 FREE NOVELS PLUS 2 FREE GIFTS!

KIMANI™ ROMANCE

Love's ultimate destination!

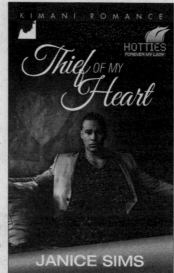

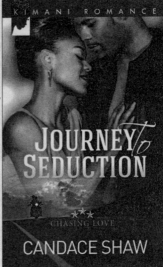